Luke's eyes were still burning, blazing down at Talia. She stared at him, breathless, heart pounding, mouth bee-stung with the naked passion in his kiss, lips parting helplessly.

"Do you see, now, why I've been the way I have to you?" The hoarseness was still in his voice. "Because it was the only way—the only way!—to stop me doing what I've just done. It was my only protection—"

His hands fell away from her, and she swayed in their absence. Blood was pounding in her ears, racing in her veins. She was dazed—crazed.

He gave that harsh, humorless laugh again. "So tell me now to go—"

His voice changed, his stance changed. The darkness in his eyes changed.

"Or tell me to stay..."

Julia James lives in England and adores the peaceful verdant countryside and the wild shores of Cornwall. She also loves the Mediterranean—so rich in myth and history, with its sunbaked landscapes and olive groves, ancient ruins and azure seas. "The perfect setting for romance!" she says. "Rivaled only by the lush tropical heat of the Caribbean—palms swaying by a silver-sand beach lapped by turquoise waters... What more could lovers want?"

Books by Julia James

Harlequin Presents

Securing the Greek's Legacy
The Forbidden Touch of Sanguardo
Captivated by the Greek
A Tycoon to Be Reckoned With
A Cinderella for the Greek
Tycoon's Ring of Convenience
Billionaire's Mediterranean Proposal

Secret Heirs of Billionaires

The Greek's Secret Son

Mistress to Wife?

Claiming His Scandalous Love-Child
Carrying His Scandalous Heir

One Night With Consequences

Heiress's Pregnancy Scandal

Visit the Author Profile page
at Harlequin.com for more titles.

Julia James

IRRESISTIBLE BARGAIN WITH THE GREEK

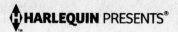
HARLEQUIN PRESENTS®

Recycling programs for this product may not exist in your area.

ISBN-13: 978-1-335-53865-9

Irresistible Bargain with the Greek

First North American publication 2019

Copyright © 2019 by Julia James

This edition published by arrangement with Harlequin Books S.A.

For questions and comments about the quality of this book, please contact us at CustomerService@Harlequin.com.

® and TM are trademarks of Harlequin Enterprises Limited or its corporate affiliates. Trademarks indicated with ® are registered in the United States Patent and Trademark Office, the Canadian Intellectual Property Office and in other countries.

Printed in U.S.A.

IRRESISTIBLE BARGAIN
WITH THE GREEK

PROLOGUE

THE BEDROOM WAS still in shadow, the thick drapes masking the early dawn outside. On feet she could hardly drag forward Talia forced herself to the door. Every cell of her body screamed in silent protest, but she made herself do what she knew she had to do.

Leave.

Leave the man sleeping in the wide bed, the bare, lean-muscled torso that she had caressed in ecstasy exposed by the half-drawn cover.

Emotion stabbed her like a knife eviscerating her insides. To walk out on him—oh, dear God—to make herself walk out on the man who had swept her off her feet, who had taken her to a paradise she had never dreamt existed! The man who had offered her for such a pitifully few blissful hours the hope of something she had never known.

Escape—blissful, wondrous escape—from the prison in which she was trapped.

The prison to which she was returning now. Because she could do nothing else.

As she turned the door handle as quietly as she could she could feel her phone vibrating yet again in her evening bag. It summoned her back home to the prison in which she had to live.

The knife twisted again. It mocked the wonders of the night she had just spent in this man's arms—how he had taken one look at her and with that single look she had known she would do what she had never done in all her life: give herself fully and rapturously to him without hesitation or doubt.

She had let him sweep her away from the party, their eyes only for each other, glorying in the sensual desire that had consumed her, that she had never known before in all her life. More—oh, surely more than only physical passion!

Another twist of the knife stabbed yet more achingly. There had been a connection between them as tangible as their bodies entwining in blazing passion in the night—something that had drawn them to each other. An ease in conversation, a natural communication that had brought smiling laughter bubbling up in her, a warmth and closeness that had been more than the physical union of their bodies…

The final twist of the knife almost made her cry out with the pain of it as she silently eased the bedroom door open, unable to tear her eyes from the man she would never see again.

Could never see again.

And now the anguish flooded through her veins, drowning her. She could never do what they had so ecstatically talked of in the long, long reaches of the night.

'Come with me!' he had said, his eyes alight. 'This night is only the start of what we shall have together! Come with me to the Caribbean—a thousand islands to explore! We'll see them all! And every single one will be for us! Come with me…'

She heard his voice, warm and vibrant, ringing in her head.

'Come with me!'

Her hand flew to her mouth to stifle the sob that rose in her throat. Impossible! It was impossible for her to go with him.

Impossible to do anything but what she was doing now.

Leaving him.

CHAPTER ONE

The previous evening

LUKE XENAKIS GLANCED up at the Victorian warehouse, converted now into highly fashionable loft apartments in the old London Docklands. He'd come here from the City, straight from that final meeting with his broker—the one that had taken him over ten long, punishing years to achieve. And now, at last—*Thee mou!*—at last he had done what he had set out to do.

Emotion speared through him, hard and vicious. Finally he was exerting his death-grip on his enemy's throat.

A life for a life.

His ancestors would have had no hesitation in making that bitter truth a literal one. Luke's mouth twisted as he entered the building. But in these more civilised days there had to be other ways to exert savage justice upon those

who so deserved it. And now—tonight—
that justice was finally being served upon his
enemy.

Within twenty-four hours the man would
be destroyed.

Wiped out financially. Ruined.

The twist in his mouth turned to a smile. A
savage smile.

He headed up the echoing iron staircase
to the topmost loft apartment, from which
he could already hear the thump of pounding music, driving all other thoughts out of
his head.

It was just what he wanted now.

The start of his new life…

Talia paused in the entrance lobby to the loft
apartment, hesitant suddenly. Should she really dive into the party inside? Then she rallied her nerve.

I need this.

Tonight, at least, for the space of a few hours
she would lose herself. Forget the pressures of
her life—pressures that were increasing all the
time, it seemed.

She sighed inwardly. She knew why. Her
poor mother's nerves were more jagged than
ever, and her father's perpetually short temper
was even shorter these last few months. Why,

Talia had no idea, and she didn't want to know. She spent all her energy trying to soothe her nervy mother and placate her tyrannical father so he would not turn on her mother.

It was wearying and stressful, but she had no option, she thought bitterly as she paused on the threshold of the party. No option but to go along with what her father wanted of her or it would be her mother who would pay the price of his vicious ill humour and displeasure.

So I have to go on being Natasha Grantham, ornamental daughter of the wildly successful property magnate Gerald Grantham, of Grantham Land. I have to be part of the image he puts out, along with his elegant, fashionable wife, his huge riverside mansion in the Thames Valley and this even more huge villa in Marbella. And the luxury apartments all over the world, the fleet of exorbitantly lavish cars, the yacht and the private jet. All of this so that others can envy his success and wealth and achievement.

It was all her father cared about—his success and his image. Certainly not about his wife and daughter.

The pitiful thing, Talia thought bleakly, was that whereas *she* was painfully aware of that bleak truth, her mother persisted in believing the fiction that he was devoted to them. She made endless excuses for him—the pressure of work, the demands of his business, he was doing it all for them. But Talia knew that her father was devoted only to one person and one cause: himself.

She and her mother were merely possessions—props to make him look good. Her mother, Maxine, was expected to be a glittering society hostess, and she was to be the decorative dutiful daughter, working for him as his interior designer, overseeing the refurbishment of his property purchases as he directed, and available on demand for the endless social functions he required her to attend. In exchange she was allowed to live rent-free in one of his many London flats, with an allowance to cover her wardrobe expenses.

Talia's eyes shadowed again. The world saw her as a pampered princess, her daddy's darling—but the reality was brutally different. She was a pawn in the ruthless power game at which her father excelled as he controlled every aspect of her life with an iron fist.

To get any time away from his demands was precious to her. Like tonight. On an impulse that was quite unlike her, she'd taken up a casually worded invitation from someone she knew in the world of interior design to come to this party. It was not her usual scene at all.

Typically, on the rare nights she had to herself, she stayed in, or occasionally went to a concert or the theatre, either on her own or with a girlfriend.

Never with a man.

She never dated. Only once had she indulged in an affair, in her early twenties, but her father had ruthlessly used his influence to ruin the young man's career, and then told Talia what he had done. She had learnt her lesson.

Now, at twenty-six, it was hard to accept that she could never indulge in a relationship of her own choosing. All around her partygoers were mingling with each other, dancing, flirting, hooking up. Restlessness filled her.

How long can I endure my life as it is?

Never had the gilded cage she lived in seemed more unbearable. Never had she felt so trapped, so stifled. Never had she felt more desperate to escape.

And tonight, dear God, she *would* escape it. She would immerse herself in the party and dance the night away. Her mother was at the Thames-side mansion, her father abroad— probably with one of his mistresses.

The longer he was away the better!

She took a breath, plunging forward. Through the crush she could see, way across the huge room, beneath the iron girder rafters of the loft apartment and the steel columns dividing up the space, an area that had been set up as a bar.

As she made her way towards it, squeezing past people, she could feel male eyes on her. It was a familiar feeling—all her life she'd known that her glorious chestnut hair, tawny eyes, fine-boned features and flawless skin were part and parcel of the image her father wanted her to present to the world, reflecting well on himself for having a beautiful ornamental daughter to show off.

Usually she dressed at his diktat, in suits and dresses that were too fussy for her own taste. But tonight she was defying his rules. She gave her head a little shake, feeling her long hair, loosened from its customary up-swept style, snaking lushly down over her bare back, framing her face. She'd used more make-up than she usually did, accentuating her eyes, her cheekbones, her rich red mouth.

The strapless dark burgundy dress she was wearing—shorter than she typically wore, and far more figure-hugging—had been an impulse purchase that afternoon, bought from a second-hand designer boutique she favoured because it helped her spend less of her allowance than her father realised, and little by little she could squirrel away some funds into a personal bank account he could not monitor. Just in case one day she could make a break for freedom…

She yanked her mind from that tantalising, though as yet hopeless dream, and focussed on reaching the bar. She could feel her hips sway as she stalked forward on vertiginous five-inch heels. Reaching the bar, she paused, resting her lavishly braceleted wrists on the downlit surface. She wanted a drink. Not to get drunk, but simply to signal to herself that tonight she was going to please herself. Let go a little. Lighten the endless crushing pressure of her life.

Live a little for herself, just for once.

'White wine spritzer, please,' she said, and smiled at the barman.

'And a sloe gin for me, please, while you're at it.'

The voice that had spoken behind her was deep and very slightly accented. She found herself half turning—and then stilled.

The man standing there was tall—easily six foot plus—and without her volition Talia felt her eyes widening in raw, female appreciation. It was an instinctive, visceral response to what she was seeing.

Dark hair, dark eyes, tough jaw, a blade

of a nose and a sculpted mouth, wide shoulders, a broad chest, narrow hips, and long, long legs...

The man's gaze flicked from the barman to her, and an even more visceral reaction swept through her. In the assessing sweep of his eyes she saw instantly—felt tangibly—that he liked what he was seeing and was making no attempt to hide it. He let his dark gold-flecked eyes rest on her almost with a sense of entitlement, and she felt an answering quiver go through her that was shocking in its intensity.

It was as if he knew she would welcome his blatant approval of her appearance. As if he knew she would return it. As if he had no idea that she was Gerald Grantham's daughter, who was never free to follow her own impulses, whatever they might be. Whatever a man like this might incite in her...

She felt a strange quiver go through her, a flush of heat rush up her body—of which she had become suddenly, vividly aware beneath his dark assessing gaze. She was conscious of the swell of her breasts, the curve of her hips, the expanse of shoulders and throat exposed to his gaze and the wanton fall of lush hair down her naked back...

She felt her breath catch—half in shock at her own uncontrollable reaction, half in unstoppable response to the way this man was looking at her. She knew her pupils were dilating as part of her instant, overpowering reaction to his physical appeal, and there was nothing she could do to disguise it.

What is happening?

The words seared across her consciousness. This was like nothing she had ever experienced! Not even with the one lover she had ever had.

She saw him complete his appraising sweep of her, and then he was reaching out a hand to close it around the ice-dewed tumbler being set down for him on the bar, raising it to his mouth in a leisurely fashion.

'To a suddenly more interesting evening,' he said, and tilted the tumbler at her.

The dark glint in his eye revealed his intentions and the tug at his mouth showed satisfaction.

For a second Talia felt something clench inside her—a kind of hollowing out that went right to the core of her and made it impossible for her to break the dark, binding hold of his eyes.

Oh, God, what has he done to make me react like this?

With a final effort she schooled her expression and, making no reply—which would have been impossible anyway, struck as she was with sudden breathlessness—reached for her wine glass, which was also now on the bar. Did her lifting of the glass make her hand tremble slightly? Or was it the after-effect of that assessing perusal?

She took a mouthful of her spritzer—a larger gulp than she'd intended. But she felt she needed it. Badly.

She realised the man was holding out his free hand towards her. He was wearing dark trousers and a white, deceptively simple shirt that she could tell was expensively tailored. It was open-necked, the cuffs turned back, exposing tanned, sinewy wrists, and he was sporting a watch she recognised as a luxury brand. Even the kind of people who frequented flashy, fashionable parties like this could not easily afford such a custom-made timepiece.

The dark eyes were resting on her still. The glint was gone, and now there was only speculation in his gaze.

'Luke,' he said, his hand still extended.

He was clearly waiting for her to respond in kind. And he seemed to have every confidence that she would.

As if of its own volition, she felt her hand take his. Felt the coolness of his fingers, the strength in them. A door seemed to be opening—a door that beckoned enticingly, alluringly.

'Talia.' She smiled.

Quite deliberately she used the name she had adopted as her own. Her father always called her Natasha, in place of her given name, Natalia, which was preferred by her mother. But 'Talia' was neither her father's dutiful imprisoned daughter nor her mother's protective guardian. 'Talia' was *herself*—and tonight… oh, tonight, on this brief, rare opportunity to *be* herself, it seemed fitting.

'Talia…'

She heard it echoed in a way that made it sound somehow more exotic, more sensual. His low voice had the trace of an accent in it, a timbre that seemed to set her vibrating at some subliminal level.

The dark glint of his eyes came her way again, and that knowing tug at his mouth. He took a considered mouthful from his glass, then set it back on the bar, letting his forearm rest on the surface. His stance altered, became relaxed.

But he wasn't relaxed. The thought flickered in her head. He was like a panther, trying not to startle its prey before it was ready to pounce.

'So, Talia, tell me about yourself.'

The invitation was casual, merely a gambit to continue the exchange. An exchange that was based, as she was so electrically aware, not on who they were but on the current that was running between them.

She paused a moment, taking another sip of wine. Should she go along with this, considering the powerful physical impact this man was having on her? *Because* of it?

Yet even as she hesitated, hovering between habitual caution and that intoxicating glimpse of freedom, she heard her own voice answer. 'I'm an interior designer,' she said.

Her voice was quite composed, she was glad to note, which was so at odds with what she was actually feeling as she sipped again at her spritzer. She saw him lift one questioning eyebrow towards the stark interior around them.

'This place, for example?' he asked.

She shook her head. 'No, this isn't my style at all!'

She glanced around the bare brick walls, the industrial RSJs exposed across the lofty roof space, the reclaimed floorboards and the spotlit modern art adorning walls.

Her eyes shadowed momentarily. Though this starkly modernist interior was not to her taste, it was true, her own style was not something she was ever allowed to express. Her father dictated exactly what he wanted her to do: produce flashy interiors that looked as if they cost a lot of money. And she was expected to produce them on a miniscule budget in order to maximise her father's profit on resale.

She hated everything she produced for her father.

No!

She would not think about her father now, nor about anything to do with the prison she lived in. Not when this amazing man was focusing on her, making her pulse quicken, making her eyes want only to gaze on him, drink him in...

'And what about you?' she heard herself asking, absorbing the way the planes of his face accentuated his looks, the way his dark eyes matched the sable of his hair—absorbing everything about him...*everything*...

He gave a slight shrug. 'Investments,' he replied.

He had said the word carelessly, but there was something in the timbre of his voice that was edged like a blade. Talia's eyes flickered uncertainly.

'You must be good at it,' she observed, her eyes slipping to the custom-made watch around his lean wrist.

He saw her glance at it. 'A present to myself today,' he said dryly.

'A very nice one!' Talia murmured, even more dryly. 'Is it your birthday?'

'Better,' he replied, taking another mouthful of his drink. 'I've just achieved something I've worked towards for more than ten years, and it's going to be a sweet, sweet moment.'

There was that same edge to his voice again, but it was more intense now. Almost…unnerving.

Not a man to cross.

'You sound very driven,' she heard herself say.

His expression stilled. 'Driven? Oh, yes…' For a moment he seemed to be looking far away, then abruptly his gaze refocused on her. 'So, what brings you here tonight, Talia?'

The unsettling note in his voice had gone and now there was only…*invitation.* Invitation in the sweep of his lashes, the slight but distinct relaxing of his pose as he helped himself to another mouthful of his drink.

She shrugged. 'What brings anyone to a party?' she countered.

That sweep of his lashes came again, as if her answer amused him. 'Do you want me to answer that?' he challenged.

Unspoken between them was the answer already. The reason so many people went to parties was to see and be seen. And to hook up...

She gave a little shake of her head, dipping it slightly to take a sip from her glass. Then, as if the wine had emboldened her, she glanced back at him. 'Is that why you're here?'

This time his lashes did not sweep down. This time his gaze was level on her. 'Perhaps,' he murmured.

His gaze lingered, telling her just why he had said that. She felt heat flush through her. Heat she was not used to. Heat that might burn her.

This is going too fast! I should back away, mingle...

But he was speaking again, draining his glass and setting it back on the counter. His eyes washed over her, and as they did so all the caution in her evaporated. She felt her pulse surge, her cheeks flush, her lips part. A heady sense of freedom—of what that freedom might offer her—was vivid within her. What this man had she didn't know. She only knew that never, ever in her life had she encountered it or experienced the impact he was having on her.

And she could not—*would* not—resist it.

Whatever is happening, I want it to happen!

'But one thing I *am* certain of,' she heard

him say, and there was that glint in his eye that told her just how certain he was, 'is that tonight calls for champagne!'

He turned to the barman and instantly two flutes were presented to them, sparkling gently. Talia took one, feeling again that heady surge in her veins.

'Is this a toast to your "sweet, sweet moment"?' she asked, lifting her glass to him, a smile flashing in her own eyes now, as they met his boldly.

For a second his hand stayed, and then he lifted his own glass to her.

'To even more,' he said.

The message was unmistakable, and it told her just what 'even more' would be.

And in her eyes was the answer she was giving him...

Luke lay, one arm behind his head, the other around Talia's slender waist. Her long hair swathed his chest and her breath was warm on his shoulder as she slept in his embrace. Sweet God, had there ever been a night in his life like this?

It was a pointless question. No woman had ever been like this one!

From the very first I knew it.

From that first moment of seeing her there,

at the bar, with her glorious hair tumbling down her bare back, her spectacular figure sheathed in that clinging dark red dress... And her face... Oh, her breathtaking beauty was so dramatic, so stunning, it had stopped him in his tracks.

Desire, instant and immediate, had fired in him—the unmistakable primitive response of a man to a woman who seared his consciousness. Whatever it was about her, it was like a homing signal, drawing him right to her.

Talia.

A woman he had known only a few short hours, but who had turned his life upside down.

He felt his arm tighten possessively around her. He had known right from the first instant that he wanted her—that she, of all the women in the world, was the one who would mark for him the start of his new life.

My old life is done. I have accomplished what I had to do: the task that was set for me the day my father died from sorrow for what had been taken from him and the day my mother died of a broken heart.

His thoughts darkened, slicing back down the long punishing years to the moment when he'd vowed to avenge his parents, who had been stripped—cheated—of everything they'd held so precious.

The stress of it had killed his father, and the man who had done that had laughed in Luke's face when, at barely twenty years old, he'd stormed into his office, raging at him, only for the cursed man to light a fat cigar with his fat fingers and summon his goons to beat up Luke, his victim's son, and throw him out on the street.

And now he is destroyed. I've taken everything from him just as he took everything from my parents. They can finally rest in peace.

And he, too, could rest now—rest from the infinite pursuit of more and yet more money, so that he could forge the weapon that would finally bring down his enemy.

Now his whole life stretched ahead of him.

He had been wondering what he should do with it, but suddenly his expression changed, softened.

In the long years of amassing his fortune, closing the net on his enemy, he had had only fleeting affairs with women who had only wanted that. Affairs that had been merely a brief respite from the dark, driven purpose of his life. Affairs that had not lasted.

I wasn't free to do anything else.

But now his long, gruelling task was accomplished, and there was nothing to keep him from finding for himself a woman who could transform his life, who could join him as he journeyed towards the bright, sunlit future that beckoned to him.

And he had found her! Instinct told him she was the one.

He drew her close, grazing her cheek with his mouth, feeling her stir in his arms. He felt a stirring in himself, too, of the desire that had burned between them—the desire that they had slaked with mutual urgency when they had left the party and he'd brought her back here to his hotel suite.

They had dined on food from room service and drunk yet more champagne. They had talked of he knew not what—except he knew that it had not been about themselves. It had been with ease and familiarity, and with a ready laughter that had seemed to spring naturally and spontaneously, as if they had known each for so much longer than a bare few hours.

And he had found her on the very night that he had finally avenged his parents by accomplishing his enemy's total destruction. He had wanted this night to be special, so that it would mark the start of his new life—the life he'd never been able to claim for himself until now—and now he knew exactly how he wanted this wonderful new life to be.

It would be spent with this woman, and this woman alone...

He felt a shuddering wonder at having found her at such a moment. He grazed her cheek again, softly and sensuously, emotion filling him. She stirred again in her exhausted sleep of passion spent, her arm around his waist tightening instinctively. His mouth moved from her cheek to her parted lips, feathering their tender contours. He felt her waking, and as he trailed a hand over the sweet mound of her breast he felt her nipple crest beneath his palm and his arousal strengthened, quickening his responsive flesh. Desire surged in him and he knew that he wanted to possess her again—to be possessed again.

His kiss deepened and she responded to him, her eyes fluttering open, full of wonder and full of desire. Full of a hunger that he was only too happy to share and sate. His body moved over hers and he murmured her name, caressing her soft, slender body, parting her slackening thighs as her arms wound around his spine. She was whispering his name, drowning in his kisses...

This second time was as glorious as the first—each reaching their climax with a shuddering intensity that swept them away in the ultimate union, an absolute fusing of their bodies. And afterwards, hearts still thudding, breathing ragged, he held her against him, her body trembling in the aftermath of ecstasy.

With a hand that was not entirely steady he smoothed back her hair. He smiled at her, his eyes lambent. But there was a seriousness in his voice behind the smile. 'You know this can't just be one night?'

Her eyes searched his. 'How can it be anything else?'

Her voice was troubled, and he needed to set her mind at rest. 'Do you not see how special this is? This night is only the start of what we shall have together.' He swooped a sudden kiss upon her mouth. 'Come with me. Come with me today—straight away, this morning!'

For an instant that troubled look was in her eye, and then, as if consciously banished, it was gone.

'Where to?' she cried out, half in humour, half in an emotion he could not name.

'Anywhere we want. Name somewhere you want to go. Anywhere at all.'

She laughed now, catching his eagerness. 'The Caribbean!' she exclaimed. 'I've never been in all my life!'

'Done!' He gave an answering laugh. 'Now

all you have to do is choose the island.' He rolled onto his back, wrapping one arm around her shoulders, the other across her flank. 'There are a thousand to choose from—we can explore them all!'

He heard her laugh again, and then he was cradling her cheek with his hand.

'Come with me.' His voice was different now. Serious. Intense. 'Come with me.'

His eyes met hers, held them. She was still gazing up at him, and the troubled look had found a home there once more.

Could she not believe that he was serious? That this was no idle banter?

He drifted his hand languorously across her silken flank and felt her stomach tauten at his sensuous touch. 'Let me persuade you,' he said huskily.

Emotion was welling up in him, as powerful as the desire building in him again. Words shaped in his mind.

I will not lose her—not now. I will not.

It was his last conscious thought as passion was rekindled between them, consuming all in its heat.

I will not lose her...

Luke stirred. Something was wrong. Very wrong. He reached out his arm, feeling only cold sheets. His eyes flared open, going immediately to the en suite bathroom door. It was standing open, no one inside. His eyes swept the room.

No Talia.

And no handbag, no shoes, no jacket, no dress. No discarded underwear slipped from her eager body as he'd taken her to his bed, to sate himself on her and change his life for ever...

No trace of her existence.

Except the note propped on the desk.

Face stark, he got up and walked towards it. Something was tightening around his guts, like a boa constrictor throwing its coils around him to crush the life from him.

Luke—I have to go. I didn't want to wake you.

That was it. Nothing else. For a long moment he just stared at it as the breath was crushed from his lungs. Then, wordlessly, he screwed it up and dropped it into the bin.

He walked into the en suite bathroom refusing to feel a single emotion.

CHAPTER TWO

TALIA SAT IN the back of the taxi, staring at her phone. It was signalling a low battery, and she was glad of it in a cowardly way. Her brain was not working properly. It seemed to be split in two, and neither side would connect with the other. She was still with Luke, folded against his body, dreaming of Caribbean islands.

Islands to escape to...islands to set me free...

Free from what her eyes were forcing into her head as she reread her mother's repeated pleading texts.

Darling, phone me! You must phone me. You absolutely must!

She could not face making the call. Yet fear was biting at her out of nowhere. Her mother had never sounded so desperate...

But before she phoned her she must get to her flat, set her phone to charge and then shower—wash Luke from her. And she must change into her day clothes—what she thought of as her prison clothes.

A shaft of anguish pierced her. She silenced it. She had to. There was no choice but to bury it way down deep. Her prison door had opened—but for a fleeting moment only. Now it was slammed shut again and that fear was biting at her.

Something was up. What could have made her mother so desperate?

The taxi driver pulled up at her apartment block and she paid him, clambering out on shaky limbs, bare feet crammed into high heels. She slipped the phone into her bag and hurried to the exterior doors of the block.

The doorman stepped towards her, holding up a hand. 'I'm sorry, Miss Grantham, but I've orders to prevent anyone entering,'

She stopped short. Stared blankly. 'Orders?' she echoed, her voice blank.

'Yes, miss,' he said. 'From the new owners.'

She tried to make sense of what he'd said. 'Someone's bought the block from Grantham's?' she said stupidly.

He shook his head, looking at her with a

touch of sympathy. 'No, miss. Someone's bought Grantham's—what's left of it.'

Talia's mother flung herself at her.

'Oh, darling, thank God—thank *God* you're here! Oh, what is happening? How did this happen?'

She was hysterical, and Talia was on the verge of hysteria herself.

How she had got herself from central London to her parents' house she hardly knew. Her brain had simply ceased to function. Now, the only thing she could do, besides tightening her arms instinctively around her clingy, crying mother, was say, 'Where's Dad?'

Her mother threw back her head. Her hair was unstyled, her make-up absent—she looked years older than she did in the carefully presented image Talia was used to seeing.

'I can't contact him!' Hysteria was present in her voice still. 'I phone and phone and nothing happens! I can't even get through to his office—it rings out! Something's happened to him. I know it has. I know it!'

Gently, Talia set her mother aside. 'I have to find out what's going on,' she said.

There was a stricken note in her own voice, and she was not sure how she was still managing to function, but she knew that above all she needed to discover what had happened to her father's company. To her father…

Five minutes on the Internet later and she knew. It was blazoned all over the financial press.

Grantham Land goes under:
LX Holdings picks over the carcass!

She read the article in shock. Disbelief. Yet her disbelief was seared with the hideous knowledge that everything was true, whatever her desperate hope that it was not. Her father's company had gone under, collapsing under a mountain of hitherto concealed debts, and all remaining assets acquired by a new owner.

Like her mother—sobbing jerkily on the sofa while Talia hunched over her laptop—Talia tried to phone through to her father's office. The call rang out, unanswered. Unlike her mother, she then tried to find a number for the company that seemed to have bought what was left of Grantham Land, but LX Holdings did not seem to exist—certainly not in the UK.

She started to search for overseas companies, but realised how little she knew of corporate matters. The press didn't seem to know much either—the adjective employed in their articles to describe the acquiring company was 'secretive'.

As for where her father was… Talia knew with bleak certainty that filled her entirely that he had gone to earth. He would not easily be found. As to whether he would bother to get in touch with his wife and daughter…

Her mouth tightened to a whip-thin line. She turned her head towards her mother, huddled in a sodden mass of exhausted hysteria. Would her father care?

She knew the answer.

No, he would not. He had abandoned them to whatever would be the fallout from this debacle.

Fallout that, within a week, she would know to be catastrophic.

Luke sat in his office. Beyond the window he could see Lake Lucerne. He had deliberately chosen this place for his base because of its very quietness.

Throughout his entire career he had striven to draw as little attention to himself as possible. The financial press called his company 'secretive' and he liked it that way. Needed it that way. He'd needed to amass the fortune he'd required for his purpose as unobtrusively as possible.

His corporate structure was deliberately opaque, with shell companies, subsidiaries in several jurisdictions, and complex financial vehicles all designed with one purpose in mind: to amass money through careful, assiduous speculation and investment without anyone noticing, and then, once his fortune was sufficiently large, to hunt his enemy to destruction.

And now his enemy was defeated. Destroyed utterly. Wiped off the face of the earth—literally, it seemed. For, like the sewer rat he was, he'd gone to ground.

Luke had a pretty shrewd idea of where he'd gone, and it was not a place where he would feel safe. Those from whom his quarry had borrowed money in his final desperate attempts to stave off the ruin rushing upon him were not likely to be forgiving of the fact that he could not repay them at all.

He tore his mind away—that was not his concern. His concern was what to do with the rest of his life.

He felt his guts twist. His face hardened with a bleakness in his expression that he could not banish.

Weeks had passed since the night that had transformed his existence—when he had so rashly thought, for those brief hours, that he had started his new life, free at last from the punishing task he had set himself. He still could not accept what she had done—could not accept how totally, devastatingly wrong he had been about her.

I thought she felt as strongly as I did! I thought what was between us was as special to her—as mind-blowing, as amazing and as lasting—as it was to me. I thought we had started something that would change our lives.

That twist in his guts came again, like a rope knotting around his midriff. Well, he had thought wrong, hadn't he? That incredible night had meant nothing to her—nothing at all.

She walked away with barely a word—just that brutal note. How could I have got it so wrong? Got her so wrong?

In the punishing years since he'd set out to wreak vengeance upon the man who had driven his father to an early grave he'd had no time for relationships—only those fleeting affairs. Was that why he'd got this woman Talia—the name echoed tormentingly in his head… *Talia*—so wrong?

What do I know of women? Of how they can promise and deceive?

With a razored breath he reached jerkily for the file lying in front of him. He flicked it

open, seeking distraction from his tormenting thoughts.

The photos inside mocked him, but he made
himself stare at them—made himself read the
accompanying detailed notes and scan down
the complex figures set out in the financial
analysis provided.

With an effort of mind he forced himself to
focus. The rest of his life awaited him. He had
better fill it somehow.

His acquisitions team were busy stripping
what flesh remained on the carcass of his prey,
disposing of any remaining assets for maximum profit—which they would do, he knew,
with expert efficiency. He had left them to it.
His goal had been to destroy his enemy, not
make money out of his destruction. He had
plenty more of the money that he'd amassed—
enough to give him a life of luxury for as long
as he lived. Now all he sought were ventures
to invest in that would be for his own enjoy-
ment. And this project, displayed in the photos
in front of him, would do as well as anything
else.

His mouth twisted and thoughts knifed in
his head. The photos showed palm trees, an
azure sea, the verdant greenery of the Caribbean.

I would have taken her there...

The thought left a hollowness in its wake, an emptiness that would not leave him.

Talia stared out of the window of the low-cost carrier's plane that was winging her to Spain. Dread filled her. Her mother was at the Marbella villa, where Talia had taken her in those first nightmare days after her father's disappearance and financial ruin.

It had been painstakingly explained to her by the blank-faced lawyer who had summoned her to her father's former City HQ, where she'd been able to see through the glass door all the deserted offices being dismantled and stripped of their furnishings by burly men. Her father's ruin encompassed not only the corporate assets, but Gerald Grantham's personal assets too.

'Your father put everything he owned into the company—initially for tax advantages and latterly to shore up the accounts. Consequently…' the man had looked impassively at Talia, who had stared back at him white-faced '…it all now passes to the acquiring owner.' He'd paused, then said unblinkingly, 'Including, of course, the riverside mansion in the Thames Valley and all its contents.'

Talia had paled even more, as the man had gone on.

'Vacant possession is required by the end of the week.'

So she'd taken her mother to Spain, thanking heaven that the villa seemed to have been spared. It appeared to be owned by a different corporation—an offshore shell company her father had set up.

In Spain, she'd tried to sort out the pathetic remnants of what they had left—which was almost nothing. All their bank accounts had been frozen, and all the credit cards. Had it not been for Talia's secret personal account—the one she'd opened in defiance of her father's diktats—she would not even have been able to buy air tickets or food. Or to pay Maria, the only member of staff in Spain she'd been able to keep on. She needed Maria as her mother's only support when she went back to London to see if there was news about anything else she could salvage.

But it had turned out to be the reverse. Now, with dread mounting in her, she knew she would have to give her mother the worst news of all. The Marbella villa was being taken from them…

They had been given a fortnight to get out, and in that time Talia was going to have to find them somewhere else to live *and* keep her mother from collapsing totally. It would finish her, she knew, to lose the villa as well as everything else—as well as her husband. Which was a loss she simply could not and would not believe.

'He'll come back to us, darling!' Her mother's pitiful words rang in Talia's ears. 'He's just sorting things out, making it all right, and then everything will be back to normal again!'

Talia knew better. Her father was not coming back. He'd saved his own skin, leaving his wife and daughter to face utter ruin.

Her mother repeated her pathetic hopes again that evening, when Talia arrived at the palatial villa, its opulence mocking her. Talia said nothing, only hugged her mother, who seemed thinner than she had ever been, her face haggard. She looked ill and Maria, taking Talia aside, expressed concern for Maxine Grantham's health.

Talia could only shake her head, feeling dread inside her at the news she must tell her mother.

She let her mother chatter on in her staccato, nervy fashion, telling her how the pool needed to be cleaned, and how Maria *had* to have help because she couldn't cope with such a huge house on her own, and that she *must* get to Rafael, in Marbella town, who was the only person she trusted with her hair, because she couldn't possibly let her husband see her with such a rats' nest when he came back—as surely he would, very soon now.

Surely Talia must have heard from her father by now, she said. For she herself had not, and she was worried sick about him, because something dreadful must have happened for him not to be in touch...

Talia put up with it as best she could, saying soothing, meaningless things to her mother. As they sat down to eat the meal Maria had prepared Talia encouraged her mother to take more than the few meagre mouthfuls that was all she seemed to want. She had to force herself to eat, too, because above all she had to keep her strength up.

I've got to keep it together—I can't fall apart! I can't!

It was an invocation she had to repeat when, after dinner, she sat her mother down in the opulent drawing room and told her she must speak to her.

'LX Holdings has made a successful claim on the offshore company which...' she took a breath '...which owns this villa. Which means...'

She faltered. Her mother's complexion had turned the colour of whey.

Talia's voice was hollow as she made herself

finish what she had to say. 'We have to move out. They're taking the villa from us as well.' Her voice broke. 'I'm so sorry, Mum. I'm so, so sorry—'

A cry broke from her mother, high and keening. And then, as if in slow motion, Talia saw her mother's expression change, her hand fly to her chest. Her whole body convulsed and she shook like a leaf.

'No! I can't! *I can't!* I can't lose this villa too! Not this too! I can't! Oh, God, I can't!'

There was desperation in her mother's voice, and then she collapsed into a sobbing, hysterical mess, clutching at Talia. But Maxine Grantham was beyond any kind of soothing… beyond anything except complete collapse.

Restlessly, Luke seized the file from his in-tray, flicked it open, and stared down at the photos it contained. He frowned. Was this really a project he should go ahead with? It would take a lot of investment, a lot of work, and the return was uncertain.

Yet there was something in the photos that called to him. The state of brutal ruination inflicted by nature that the photos showed echoed across the years. Not earthquake damage this time, as in his memories, but the terrifying force of wind destroying whatever stood in its path.

His thoughts were bitter. Taking on such a project halfway across the world would help him put out of his mind what kept trying to occupy it—the infernal memory he needed to banish.

She didn't want me—didn't want what I wanted. Didn't want anything about me.

He cut the endless loop that wanted to play and play inside his head and went back to staring at the photos, making himself read the notes compiled for him by his agent. He needed something to fill the emptiness inside him now that his enemy was destroyed and the burning ambition that had driven him all his adult life had been finally fulfilled.

The low ring of the phone on his desk interrupted his concentration and he reached for the handset absently. It was his PA, and her voice was uncertain.

'There is someone here, Mr Xenakis, who is asking to see you. She has no appointment, and will not give her name, but she is very insistent. I told her it was impossible, but—'

Luke cut across her. He had no interest in whoever it was. 'Send her away,' he said curtly. 'Oh, and is my flight booked and the villa reservation made?'

'Yes, of course, Mr Xenakis, it is all done.'

'Good. Thank you.'

He dropped the phone down on the desk, but as he did so there was a loud noise by the door to the outer office and it was suddenly flung open. The voice of his PA was protesting vigorously in English, not the French in which she spoke to Luke.

His head shot up, anger spiking at the intrusion. But the emotion died instantly when he saw who was pushing through the open door, his PA behind her, trying to stop her.

She stopped dead.

For a second there was complete silence, even from his PA. Then Luke spoke.

'Leave us.'

But it was his PA he addressed. Not the woman who had forced herself into his office.

Not Talia.

Blankness filled Talia's mind, wiping out every turbid emotion that had been raging inside her head since she had left Marbella that morning. With Maria's help she'd got her wildly sobbing mother to bed and summoned her doctor. He'd prescribed a sedative, then taken Talia aside. He'd told her with a frown that such upset was not good for his patient, known to him already for her nervous attacks and for her weakened heart.

Talia had been appalled by the latter—her mother had never told her. The doctor had also made it clear to her that he blamed the slimming pills she took constantly. They'd put a strain on her heart—now exacerbated by her hysterical collapse.

'She must have complete rest and quiet— and no further upset!' the doctor had told Talia sternly. 'Or the consequences could be most dangerous to her! Her heart cannot take any more stress of this nature!'

Talia had shown him out, his words mocking her with a cruelty that she could scarcely bear. *No further upset...*

She'd felt a beading of hysteria herself— they were about to be evicted from the last place that Talia had so desperately hoped might be salvaged from the debacle of her father's ruin and disappearance. How could she *possibly* avoid further upset?

Throughout the sleepless night that had followed, during which she had tossed and turned, her hands clenching convulsively as she'd gazed tensely at the darkened ceiling, it had become clear that only one option was left to her.

Before she'd told her mother, her bleak plan

had been to use the fast-dwindling amount of money she'd secretly squirrelled away to rent a tiny flat, somewhere in a cheap part of the *costas*, and then get the first job she could find to bring in a salary, however meagre. Her mother would be appalled, but what else could she do?

But if she insisted on that now, after the doctor's grim warnings, she would be risking her mother's life by forcing her to leave the villa and abandoning all hope.

By morning, dull-eyed and heavy-hearted, and filled with a kind of numb, dreadful resignation, Talia had come to the only conclusion she could. After her bleak exchanges with the lawyers in London, when they'd told her she and her mother were penniless and homeless, she had finally tracked down the headquarters of the mysterious LX Holdings. A morning flight had brought her here.

And now, paralysed by shock and disbelief, she was standing in the doorway of the huge office she had forced her way into in sheer desperation.

It could not be—it could *not* be…

Luke? But how—? Why—?

Shocked words fell from her frozen lips. 'I don't understand—'

With a curt gesture he dismissed his PA who

backed away, closing the door as she left. She saw him step towards her. Heard him speak.

'Talia…'

There was a hoarseness in his voice but his face was closed, filled with tension.

'Why did you come here? *How?*' The questions shot from him like bullets.

Talia felt her face work, but speaking was almost impossible. Two absolutely conflicting realities echoed in her head. Then slowly, as the hideous truth dawned on her, she made the connection—forced herself to make it.

'It can't be—*you* can't be…' Her voice was faint. Her face convulsed again. 'You *can't* be LX Holdings—'

She saw Luke's brows snap together, as if what she'd said made no sense. His mouth twisted. 'How did you find me?' he said. He looked at her. 'How did you know?' he demanded. He had said nothing of his identity to her that fateful night—no more had she told him hers. So how…?

'They…they told me. Your lawyers in London. When they spoke to me.'

Her voice was staccato, shock thinning her words. He was still staring back at her as if what she'd said made no sense at all. Her face worked again.

'I'm Natasha Grantham,' she said.

CHAPTER THREE

LUKE FELT THE world reel. He heard her words—how could he not?—but he felt only denial slice through him. No, he would *not* let her be that! *Anyone* but that!

She was speaking still, and he could still hear her—hear her and want only to silence her.

'I'm Gerald Grantham's daughter. You've taken everything he possessed. But…but I'm asking you not…not to take the Marbella villa as well. That…that's why I've come here.'

Her voice faltered and she fell silent.

He stilled, and now a new emotion filled him—one that was cold, like ice water.

'You are Gerald Grantham's daughter?' he repeated.

He had to be sure. In his head skimmed fractured memory from long years ago, when he'd first set himself to studying everything he could about the man he was going to destroy. Grantham had a daughter, yes, and a wife, too—always being trotted out at his side, dressed to the nines, glittering with jewellery, frequenting expensive venues, spending his ill-gotten money.

What had been the wife's name? Marcia? Marilyn? Something like that…

And the daughter?

He felt that ice water fill his veins, heard her faltering voice echo in his pounding head, forced the connection through his brain. Natasha, she had said.

Logic clicked. Natasha. Wasn't that a diminutive of Natalia? Talia…?

Talia!

Savage emotion seared through him, but he quenched it with the ice-cold water in his veins. His eyes rested on hers but they were masked, letting nothing show in them. He saw her nod and lick her lips. Those full, passionate lips that had caressed his body in ecstasy.

And all along she had been the daughter of the man he had spent his adult life seeking to destroy…

The irony, as savage as the emotion shredding his brain right now, was unbearable. How could the woman who had burned across his life so incandescently, so briefly, turn out to be the daughter of Gerald Grantham?

He tore his mind away. Focussed only on the present. Ruthlessly he slammed control over himself, refused to let any part of the emotion tearing across him show. There was no expression in his eyes and his body was taut and tense.

'And you have come here wanting to keep the villa in Marbella?' He echoed her words, his voice as impassive as his face.

He saw her nod again, as if her neck were stiff.

For one long, endless moment he just looked at her, fighting for control as the shock of her identity rampaged through his consciousness. He studied her as she stood in front of him, her stance rigid, clearly as shocked as he, and hiding it a lot less well.

Deliberately he let himself take in everything about her. She was wearing a suit in dark aubergine, a designer number, though too fussily styled to show her to her best advantage. Her glorious hair was confined to a plait, her make-up was subdued, and he thought she looked thinner than when he had seen her at that party.

He considered what had caused that: the sudden poverty she'd been plunged into... the complete reversal of her circumstances... What a blow that must have been to her.

Talia Grantham.

The name was like a dead weight around his neck. Gerald Grantham's daughter—the gilded, pampered daughter of his enemy.

She was that all along and I didn't know.

The realisation, coming as it had out of the blue, was like a savage blow to his guts, doubling him up with the force of it.

And now she was here, in a designer outfit Gerald Grantham's money had bought for her, wanting to go on living in a palatial villa on an exclusive gated estate in the rich man's playground of Marbella. As if she had every right to do so. Every expectation that of *course* she could go on living there.

Gerald Grantham's daughter—taking the world for granted. Taking what she wanted just as her father had. Splashing his money on herself—money that had been bled from her father's victims.

He could feel another emotion beginning to mount in him. It was an emotion he knew well, that had fuelled the last ten years of his life: slow, low-burning, inexorable anger.

But he would not let it show. Instead he went back to his desk and threw himself into his chair, swinging to look directly at her. As he gazed at her, taking in her presence a bare few metres from him, yet another emotion rose in him, just as powerful as his anger.

It was the emotion that had first kicked through every vein in his body as his eyes had rested on her at that fateful party. And it was instant, immediate, and impossible to deny. Impossible then and impossible now.

Thee mou, how beautiful she is!

It turned out nothing could change that— nothing! Not even the hideous discovery of who she really was and why she had come here.

Not to find me again—not to seek me out after abandoning me that morning, after that unforgettable night together. No, not for that—

Anger rose within him, cutting across the sudden overwhelming longing that was flooding through him as she stood before him, so incredibly, savagely beautiful. She was having exactly the same effect on him that she had had from his very first moment of seeing her, desiring her...

Turbid emotion filled him, mingling anger and desire, and it was a toxic, dangerous mix. It was impossible to subdue. It steered him now, formed the thoughts that swirled wildly in his head—thoughts he should not be having.

I should send her packing. I should tell her

to get out of my office and get out of this villa she wants to keep for herself. I should have nothing more to do with her. She is my enemy's daughter and she walked out on me as if I were nothing to her.

He could hear the words in his head and knew what they were telling him. It was the only sane thing to do.

But the words that came out of his mouth were not those words. He lifted his hands, as if making an accommodating gesture. 'Very well,' he said. 'I don't see why not.'

Even as he spoke the words he regretted them. But he could not call them back—would not. Something was starting to burn within him—a slow fire he knew he should extinguish to prevent it rekindling the passion he felt for her.

At his words he saw her expression lighten. He smiled and went on. 'I am prepared to offer you a short-term lease—say three months—while you make alternative arrangements for your accommodation.'

He spoke briskly, in a businesslike fashion, watching her all the time.

He could see her eyes lighting up, see the visible relaxation of her stance at his reassuring agreement to what she'd come here wanting. She was getting what she wanted, despite what she had done to him.

His expression changed, becoming bland—deliberately, calculatingly so. 'I'll have a lease drawn up and rent set. I would think, given the size and location of the villa, something like thirty thousand euros a month should cover it.'

He watched her face whiten. Her reaction—such obvious outrage at his reply—made the anger inside him spear him again. But he would not let it show. Instead he smiled again, though it did not reach his eyes.

'In life, Ms Grantham,' he said, his voice silken, 'we cannot have what we cannot pay for.'

He pushed his chair back, the movement abrupt. He stood and gave a shrug of deliberate indifference.

'If you can't pay the rent you must vacate the villa,' he spelt out bluntly.

His eyes never left her, never showed any expression. Even though they wanted to sweep over her glorious body, concealed as it was beneath that fussy over-styled outfit she was wearing. It didn't suit her—however expensive it had been.

Absently, he wondered at its difference in style from the simple yet stunning dress she'd worn at that party. He wrenched his thoughts away from where they must not go. His eyes from where they must not go either...

He saw her expression change, as if her own self-control was very near the edge. It must be a shock to her, he found himself thinking, bitterness infusing his every thought and his mouth thinning. Daddy's darling daughter, realising her pampered lifestyle was over, that her doting father was no longer there to grant her every whim and wish.

'No!'

He heard her cry out in protest at his brutal spelling out of the harsh truths of life, saw her face working.

'Everything else has gone—but not that... not the villa too!'

For a moment so fleeting that Luke thought he must have misheard there seemed to be real fear in her voice, real despair...real desolation. She was staring at him, her expression pinched, and he thought he caught something vulnerable in the way she stood there, as if life had dropped a weight on her that she could not shoulder.

He felt a different emotion rise within him—one that made him suddenly want to blurt out that of *course* she could stay in the damn villa, that he didn't give a damn about any rent. It made him want to surge to his feet, close the distance between them, take her into his arms and hold her close, to tell her he would make everything all right for her, all right for them both, that he never wanted to lose her again.

But then it was gone. She was only repeating what she'd said before, just more insistently. As if she was assuming, taking it for granted.

Of course she was Gerald Grantham's daughter, was she not? She had never had to think of paying for anything at all. A rich man's princess of a daughter, who got everything she wanted handed to her on a plate by an indulgent father.

'I absolutely *cannot* lose the villa! I just can't!' Her eyes flared suddenly, widening as her long lashes swept down.

His mouth tightened again at the declaration of entitlement in her words. Her protest should have been like a match to his anger, and yet it gave rise to a quite different emotion. It was an emotion he should not let himself be feeling, but his eyes, his senses, were hungry to revisit it.

Memory flooded over him. The last time his eyes had held her she had been lying naked in his arms, sated from passion, her skin like silk against his body, her hair a glorious swathe across his shoulders, her mouth pressed against the wall of his bare chest, her exhausted limbs tangled with his...

And yet when he'd awoken from the overpowering sleep that had claimed him she had been gone, vanished into thin air.

Only to reappear now, suddenly, seemingly out of nowhere.

I can't let her walk out on me again...

The words were inside his head and he knew he should wipe them away. He knew he should send her packing. He knew exactly what he should say to Gerald Grantham's daughter.

He knew it. But he could not say it. Not for all the will in his body and in mind.

Instead, as if he were possessed by a force he could not resist, he felt his muscles start to loosen, his shoulders ease back, and then he heard the words that came from his mouth. Words he knew with every rational part of his mind he should not be saying, but which were coming from a place inside him where reason held no sway. There was only an instinct as old as time itself and just as powerful.

Not to let her walk out on him again...

'Then perhaps,' he heard himself saying, 'we can come to an alternative arrangement...'

* * *

Talia stared at him. Her senses were reeling. She was floored...in shock...mesmerised.

She had thrust her way into this inner sanctum to which that snooty PA had been determined to bar her entry, and then, as she'd stared at the man jolting to his feet at her entry, she had realised just who it was who stood before her. It was impossible to recover from this truly unexpected outcome.

She could barely countenance the brutal demand he'd made of her to pay rent in order to stay on in their own home, though she did understand on a rational level that the villa was part of the spoils of his acquisition of what was left of her father's once mighty business empire.

She had tried to ignore the leap in her senses as her eyes had clung to him in the custom-tailored suit that sheathed his lean body, the dark tie with the discreet gold tie pin, the gold links at his cuffs, the leather strap of that exorbitantly expensive watch she'd noticed the night they'd met. Still, his long-limbed pose was lithe and it radiated power—the kind of power that came from wealth, the way her father's had.

Yet Luke—*Luke Xenakis*, she reminded herself forcibly, of XL Holdings—had pursued

her father's ailing company with a power that
had nothing to do with his wealth. A power
that he could exert over her with a mere flick
of those dark lidded eyes, a twist of that sensual mouth...

She felt herself almost swaying as memories assaulted her: his arms tightening around
her, his mouth opening hers to his, his hands
gliding over her body that had trembled at his
silken touch...

With a silent groan she tore her mind away.
What use were those memories here, in this
austere office, with its views out over the gla-
cial alpine lake and the jagged, snow-capped
mountains soaring all around, as icy as the
coldness in the eyes that had once burned with
heat for her?

She felt something wither inside her under
the cold indifference of his gaze, and knew
she must banish from her memory the night
she had spent with him, with this man she had
given herself to so gloriously and so freely—
the man who had thrown open the gate of her
prison, offering her a beguiling glimpse of the
freedom and bliss that could be hers.

As always, her prison doors had closed on
her and were still shut. For now, as then, her
first responsibility must be to her mother, to
protect her from the catastrophe that had en-

gulfed them with her father's ruin. She must protect her from blows she could not cope with yet, and soften the final blow of losing her last refuge from the bleak poverty she was going to have to face.

She knew she must not run from Luke in an effort to try to end the torment of seeing him again and feeling his coldness towards her, and nor should she throw herself at him to beg him to listen to *why* she'd had to leave him as she had, though she desperately wanted to do both. She must accept whatever he offered her if it helped protect her mother just a little longer.

She forced herself to focus on what he was saying, to try to make sense of it. 'What... what do you mean?'

She saw a veil come down over his eyes—another layer of inscrutable protection. He was so close to her and yet so infinitely far away. Something ached inside her at the distance between them now. With every instinct in her being she knew that he had not forgiven her for walking out on him that morning, leaving him after such a night as they had shared.

For a moment she wanted to cry out, to tell him *why* she had left like that, to try and make him understand that her life had never been hers to live as she wanted.

That it still wasn't.

Whatever 'alternative arrangement' Luke had in mind, she'd have to go along with it—if it was the only way to let her mother go on living at the villa she had no choice. She had to buy the time that she so desperately needed to get her mother to face the brutal truth of how they had to live now—time to find a cheap place to move to, to get herself a job and earn money for the food they were going to eat from now on...

Her tired mind fogged as she made herself listen to what he was saying.

'I may have a job for you.'

She frowned.

'You told me you were an interior designer,' he went on. 'Are you only residential or do you have commercial experience?'

She blinked, remembering instantly the conversation they'd had, brief though it had been, as they'd introduced themselves to each other.

But we left out the most important information.

She gave a slight nod, swallowing with a dry throat.

'Very well. In that case, I'm embarking on a new business venture—a potential refurbishment project—your skills might come in useful to me. If so...' he was watching her speculatively through those veiled lashes of his '... I would accept your work in lieu of rent—if that is agreeable to you.'

Talia stared. The hope that had flared so pathetically briefly when he had first said there would be no problem in her staying on at the villa—before naming his price for that—sparked into life again.

'Yes! Yes, of course—'

The words were out of her mouth before she could stop them. The fact she would be working for the man who had brought down her father, who now owned everything that he had once possessed, was irrelevant.

She saw him sit back, cross one leg over the other and steeple his long fingers—fingers that had once trailed through her loosened hair and skimmed the contours of her naked body...

She dragged her mind away and stifled the inner voice that was telling her she was insane even to *think* of working for a man she had spent such a night with and who was now regarding her as nothing more than an employee.

But I have no choice in the matter. If he is offering me a job I have to take it—I have to! If it lets Mum stay on in the villa... If it buys me time...

She swallowed again. 'When…when do I start?'

She watched him smooth a hand over his thigh in a controlled, leisurely fashion, his eyes never leaving her, revealing nothing of what might be behind that leaden gaze.

'I'm flying out at the end of the week. Meet me at Heathrow,' he informed her.

Consternation filled Talia's face. 'Flying out? Where?'

'The Caribbean. I'll be there a fortnight—so will you.'

Violently, she shook her head. *A fortnight?* 'I couldn't! Impossible!'

It would be impossible to spend two weeks with Luke—and in the very place they had fantasised about that night together. About running away to a sun-drenched tropical island, a palm-fringed beach, with no cares or responsibilities or prison doors to stop her…

The cruelty of it mocked her. Mocked her with the torment of the prospect of having to be with him again as he was now—so cold, so distant…

She saw him shrug again—a gesture of indifference. And that was all he felt for her now, she knew.

'In which case be out of the Marbella villa next week.'

Talia shut her eyes as if she could shut out the reality of this situation. How could she turn down this offer he was making her? She couldn't. She had no choice.

Luke was speaking again. 'You can have twenty-four hours to make your decision. Phone my PA when you've made it.'

He uncrossed his legs, extending them under the wide mahogany desk, and reached for his keypad. Talia swallowed. It was a signal that she was being dismissed.

Numbly, she walked from the office.

Behind her, Luke lifted his gaze as she walked out. She could not have spelt out more clearly how repugnant she found the notion of spending time with him.

Memory stabbed at him again of how they had talked on that amazing, unforgettable night together, sated with passion, wound in each other's arms. Talked of taking off to the Caribbean together...

But it had never happened, had it? She had never had the slightest intention of going anywhere with him, of spending a single further night with him.

She used me—and left me. Had what she wanted of me and walked out.

As the door closed behind her his face darkened. Was he clinically insane to have offered her a job? Actually invited her to go with him to the place that mocked him in his taunting memories? Why the hell had he done it?

Answers stirred in the deep recesses of his mind but he silenced them. They were too dangerous to acknowledge.

CHAPTER FOUR

CAREFULLY, TALIA SAT herself down in the wide leather first-class seat on the plane, feeling tense and strained. Luke had taken the window seat and had immediately snapped open his laptop. He was taking as little notice of her as he had when she'd joined him in the First-Class Lounge, where he had merely glanced at her and nodded briefly.

Inside her chest she could feel her heart thudding. Seeing him again, even knowing who he was and what he had done, was still an ordeal.

But it's an ordeal I'm going to have to bear. I have to bear it just as I have to bear everything else. Because I don't have any choice in the matter.

She didn't—and she knew she didn't. She had known all through that gruelling twenty-four hours Luke had allowed her to make her decision that there was only one answer she could give. She had to take his job offer. If it was the only way to stop herself and her mother being summarily evicted from the Marbella villa she had to take it. That was all there was to it.

And when she'd broken the news to her mother she had only felt that decision reinforced.

As she fastened her seat belt she deliberately made herself remember the expression on her mother's face when, on her return from Switzerland, she'd sat down on her mother's bed and told her that they could stay on in the villa for the time being. As her mother's fearful and haggard face had lit with relief Talia had gone on to tell her the exciting news that she'd been offered an interior design job. The only downside was that it would take her to the Caribbean for a fortnight.

Her mother's expression had faltered momentarily, then she had rallied. 'You mustn't worry about me a bit! Maria will look after me while you're away. And it's just what you need—a chance to use your talents! I'm sure you'll have a lovely time—it won't be *all* work, will it? Oh, I do envy you!' Maxine Grantham's eyes had softened. 'It's *such* a romantic place, the Caribbean! Of course your father never liked it...'

Her voice had wavered for a moment, and then she'd become momentarily reminiscent.

'I had a boyfriend once, you know, when I was a teenager. He talked of sailing to every island there—' She had broken off, then made her tone suddenly hopeful. 'Oh, my darling, perhaps you'll meet someone special there! Oh, that would be *too* wonderful! To be romanced beneath a tropical moon!'

Talia had changed the subject, but she'd not been able to banish her mother's words from her head.

'Romanced beneath a tropical moon...'

Memory had struck her again—but they were memories of what had never happened. She had never flown off with Luke that morning after their searing night together—never fled with him as she had so longed to do.

She had felt her thoughts shift and rearrange themselves. If she took this job with him, flew to the Caribbean... Hope, like a beguiling spirit, had welled within her. Was it possible? Could it be possible...?

Could I have a second chance with him? Dare I hope for the romantic escape we should have had?

She had felt hope strengthen, take wings. Longing had filled her.

Yet now, as she sat beside him on the plane,

only anguish filled her. Her mother's words mocked her. Indeed, her own longings were mocking her.

At her side, Luke was focussed on his laptop, a faint frown of concentration between his eyes, clearly not paying the slightest heed to her presence. She felt the anguish stab at her. She knew she must subdue these dangerous, forbidden thoughts that came unbidden, but they were impossible to banish—especially the one thought that lingered, with a temptation that she felt clinging to her like a fine mesh of gold.

What if being in the Caribbean with Luke could bring them together again? What if what had happened after that party could happen again? What if he turned to her now and, instead of cold indifference, she saw in his eyes the warmth she longed for…?

'Champagne, madam?'

A stewardess was hovering with pre-flight drinks. With a start, Talia shook her head, taking an orange juice instead. Luke merely waved the tray away, not even looking up. That ache of anguish came again, silencing the pointless flare of hope that had fluttered so uselessly just a second ago.

With a silent sigh, she reached for her paperback, wanting her thoughts silenced, wanting to be diverted by something—anything that might get her through what lay ahead.

Hope was impossible—only torment was certain. Torment and regret.

I threw it away. I threw away my chance of seizing the happiness he promised me. And I walked out back to my prison.

The print in the paperback hazed and blurred. But what use was it for her to weep for what she had done? She had had to do it— nothing else had been possible.

Bleakly, she went on reading, numbing herself as best she could through the long flight. Luke barely spoke to her, and she was grateful—and yet his silence hammered nail after nail into her, showing her just how great was the distance between them.

No trace of intimacy. No trace of anything at all.

The same impersonal indifference continued once they had landed, and Talia spent the journey from the airport gazing out through the window of the chauffeur-driven car they'd climbed into.

The lush green of the island entranced her, along with the vivid glow of the setting sun, and when, after forty minutes or so, the car wound its way along a paved drive to draw up at a large house, she was happy to get out and gaze around her, feeling the humid warmth engulf her like a soft cashmere shawl after the chill of the climate-controlled car interior.

'Oh, this is beautiful!' she could not stop herself exclaiming as she gazed around at the lush gardens, with splashes of vivid colour from the tropical flowers all about.

She got no acknowledgement from Luke, who was striding indoors, so she followed him in. She'd wondered if they were heading for a hotel, but this was clearly a private villa. The large atrium-style hall reached up to high rafters, a reception room opened beyond, and there was a mahogany staircase sweeping upstairs. Staff appeared out of nowhere, murmuring in an island lilt, taking their suitcases upstairs, and Talia's bulky portfolio case and art kit.

She hesitated, not knowing what she should do, and Luke, striding towards a door at the side of the hall, turned his head.

'We'll be dining in an hour. Don't keep me waiting.'

It was all he said before he disappeared into a room in which Talia could glimpse a desk and IT equipment. He shut the door behind him with a decisive click.

With a sigh, Talia followed the luggage upstairs.

Bleakness filled her, and a weariness that came not only from the long flight. It went much deeper than that...

I've lost him—lost him for ever... And I must abandon any hope of winning him back.

She had to accept what Luke was making so chillingly clear—he had no interest in her any longer. Not as the woman she'd been at that party. There could be no second chance.

Wearily, she showered and started to get ready. A maid had unpacked for her, and as Talia selected a dress to wear she deliberately chose one her father had approved of. He had always wanted her to wear only fussy, over-styled clothes, and this knee-length dress in a pastel shade of pale blue did not suit her—but it would signal to Luke that she was well aware she was no longer of any personal interest to him. From now on she must remember that she was here only to work. Nothing more than that.

A tightness clutched around her heart, but there was nothing she could do about it.

He doesn't want me any more.

That was the truth—bleak, unvarnished—and she had to face it.

Luke sat at the head of the long table in the villa's dining room, his gaze focusing down

the table to where Talia was sitting, immobile
and expressionless. His face tightened. Inside
him he felt the emotions he'd become all too
familiar with, scything inside him. How could
he still find her so beautiful?

Just as she had that day in his office in Lucerne, she looked nothing like the way she had
at that party—there was no wanton wildness
about her at all, no tightly sheathed body, no
exposed shoulders and bare arms, no swaying
walk from five-inch heels.

Now, she was dressed for the evening, in
a knee-length cocktail dress that was high-
necked and long-sleeved—as if, he thought
with an illogical spurt of anger, she were deliberately hiding her figure from him. Her hair
was caught in the same plain coil at the back
of her head that it had been in on the flight,
and she had not put on any make-up, let alone
jewellery.

A thought flickered in his mind. *Maybe
there wasn't any jewellery left for her to
wear...*

After all, she couldn't even afford to pay
rent on a single one of Gerald Grantham's
many properties. There probably wasn't much
jewellery these days.

She would be feeling the lack of it.

His eyes flickered over her, unconsciously

changing her concealing gown to something much more to his taste. Something that would show her voluptuous cleavage, ripe for adornment with something glittering and expensive.

He tore his mind away. She wasn't here to look alluring. That was the last thing he should want her to do. It had been hard enough to have her sitting beside him hour after hour on the flight over and make himself blank her presence. It had been next to impossible not to turn his head and drink in that beauty that had caught his breath as it did again now, even when she was wearing the unflattering dress. But he must not yield to such a dangerous temptation.

She's here to work, to earn the right to go on living in a villa she can no longer afford.

It was time to remind her of that. Even more, to remind himself.

The staff were setting plates in front of them and pouring wine as Luke spoke. 'I'll be visiting the site first thing tomorrow morning,' he said abruptly, lifting his fork and starting to eat. He was hungry after the change in time zone and it was past midnight on his body clock. 'Because of the heat and the jet lag we'll make an early start.'

He saw her swallow and take a drink from

her glass. 'Where is the site?' she asked. 'And what kind of property is it?'

It seemed to be an effort for her to speak, and that annoyed him. Why *she* should be radiating tension on all frequencies was beyond him. She was the one who'd rejected him. It had been *her* choice to leave, not his.

It was pointless to wonder, yet again, whether he was clinically insane to have brought her out here with him. He'd oscillated continuously in the twenty-four hours he'd given her to make her mind up, between cancelling his impulsive offer and raising the stakes on it. When she'd walked up to him in the airport lounge he'd felt that toxic mix of emotion writhe in him again, and he'd been plunged into confusion once more.

It filled him still, but he was hammering it down, refusing to face it. He *had* been insane to bring her here—truly mad to subject himself to her presence—but it was too late to change his mind. She was here and he would have to deal with it. Whatever strength of mind it took, he had to make this Caribbean project work and then get on with the rest of his life.

I can make myself indifferent to her. I can expose myself to her presence and get her out of my damn system.

His jaw set. That was what he must focus on. This time *he* would set the finish date: she'd stay here for a fortnight, work solidly to pay her rent, and would leave when he dismissed her. This time *he* would call the shots—not her.

And by the time she left—had been dismissed by him—he would have worked her out of his system. She would mean nothing to him and he would watch her being despatched from his life, on his terms, with all the indifference he was currently trying to present to her. But by then it would be genuine indifference—not the feigned, deliberate impassivity he was treating her with now.

He answered her finally, in the same clipped tone of voice he'd used for all their brief exchanges so far.

'It's a hotel in the south of the island, where the Caribbean coastline meets the Atlantic. It's where the hurricanes hit if they reach this far. As they did last year.'

She'd started to eat, but looked up as he spoke.

He went on dryly. 'Don't worry, we're out of hurricane season now. But last year the tip of the island was struck by a particularly vicious one—climate change is, as you probably know, fuelling their force and their frequency. The area we're visiting got a hammering.'

'Is the hotel still worth refurbishing?' she asked frowningly.

'That's what I'm checking out,' he said. Dryness had turned to terseness.

She was speaking again, her voice diffident, as if she were unsure whether to speak at all, and that irritated him more.

'How badly damaged is it?' she asked.

'The external construction has borne up well—it was built to resist wind shear. But the interior has been blasted totally. It needs complete renovation.'

For the first time there was a spark of animation in her face, lightening her features. 'What do you have in mind?' she asked.

Luke's mouth thinned. 'Surprise me,' he said flatly.

He was aware that he was supressing a stab of emotion he did not want to allow admittance. That the spark of animation in her expression which had brightened her eyes, giving her a glow for the first since she'd joined him in the airport lounge, had kicked at something inside him. For a few seconds she had looked as she had that first evening— with her eyes alight, responding to him, desiring him...

He repelled the memory. No point remembering that night, however much it hammered in his brain. It was over. Done. It wasn't coming back.

She was replying. 'I have to work to the client's brief,' she said tightly. There was no animation in her reply to his crushing rebuff.

Her father, the only client she'd been allowed to have, had been exacting in his briefs, and she had learnt long ago not to challenge him on what he wanted, or even suggest any modifications. Her father had not wanted creative input—he'd wanted docile compliance. She had produced only what he'd wanted, whatever her own opinions.

'Well, my brief to you is to come up with your own ideas,' Luke said indifferently.

Talia subsided, focussing once more on her meal. From the far end of the table Luke watched her close down again as she continued eating, and he said nothing more to her. She looked tired, he realised, and he felt the same way himself, jet lag having settled in.

When coffee arrived, Luke addressed her again. 'We'll make an early start for the site visit tomorrow morning before the day heats up too much. Wear suitable clothing—shoes for walking, not posing.' He paused, wanting to make the point clear. 'Remember you are here to WORK, Talia, if you want to stay on at the villa in Marbella.'

He saw her tense at the sharpness of his reminder, and something more. Had that been *fear* he'd just seen flash in her eyes? But why should it? He almost asked the question, his expression softening instinctively. Then that blank-eyed look was back in her face, expressing only tiredness.

'Finish your coffee and go to bed,' he instructed.

She did not need to be told twice. Draining her cup, she made her escape, heels clicking on the tiled floor. Luke watched her hurry out and that now familiar jab of anger came again.

She couldn't wait to get away from him, could she?

It wasn't the first time she hadn't been able to wait to get away from him, was it?

The memory only reinforced his determination to use her presence in order to become indifferent to her.

But what if it makes you want her more...?

Talia stared around her at the scene of devastation. There were palm trees felled by the hundred-mile-an-hour winds that had uprooted them like matchsticks, and the ground was strewn with branches and vegetation, including seaweed and sand from the beach.

The hotel itself looked as if it had been blasted. Roof tiles lay smashed on the ground, window frames were hanging loose, mosquito screens falling off. She was glad that she was wearing strong rubber-soled shoes and long olive green trousers. There was shattered glass in places, too, and thick palm fronds with sharp edges.

Silently, Luke handed her a hard hat, donning one himself.

'Take care,' was all he said to her as he headed indoors.

He'd taken little notice of her on the way here—this time in a high-wheeled four-by-four—just as he had the previous day. It was as if he were blanking her deliberately, and she could do nothing but accept it—and respond in kind. She was grateful, if nothing else, that she was able to mirror his obvious indifference to her. He was treating her as someone he'd hired to do a job of work for him. Nothing personal…nothing intimate.

There was a heaviness inside her that was not just tiredness or jet lag. It had been so stupid of her to have any idiotic hope that Luke might be willing to make a fresh start with her. No, whatever they'd had was over. All that was important now was earning the rent to keep her mother at the villa at Marbella. The doctor's warning meant she could not risk her mother's health—she was too fragile, in body and mind. And her dangerously weakened heart—

She sheered her mind away, felt anguish slicing through her with a painful jagged edge.

She had lost all claim to anything personal with Luke. That was all over now—brief as it had been. She'd walked out on him. Now all she was to him was a temporary employee. And that was what she had to remember. She was here to sell her interior design skills in exchange for rent, that was all.

Keep it professional. He doesn't want anything else than that. He's made that brutally clear.

As she trailed after him, picking her way through the debris, and then stepped inside the building, she heard herself gasp in shock and dismay at the ravages within. Furniture was overturned, curtains were hanging off their rails, crockery was smashed, and there was a fetid smell of hot, humid, overpowering damp. The place had clearly been drenched, both by the pounding rain and the storm-surge of the sea, and even in the months since the hurricane it had not dried out.

She followed Luke across the huge atrium, her heart sinking at the destruction all around her, stepping carefully through the debris on the floor—bits of furniture, shards of crockery, shreds of curtains, wind-strewn sand— gritty under the soles of her shoes. Dismay filled her. How could anyone think to make something of this place again? Surely the wreckage was complete and it was impossible to restore?

All she wanted to do was get out of there as fast as she could. There was nothing worth saving. The whole place was rotting.

Gingerly, watching every step she took across the littered broken flooring, trying not to inhale the gagging smell of damp and decay, she made her way towards the arching curve of the far side of the atrium where it opened onto the gardens—or what had once been the gardens.

Avoiding a louvered ceiling-height shutter, hanging from its hinges, she stepped out onto the terrace beyond, lifting her eyes and blinking in the bright light after the odoriferous gloom of the interior.

And her breath caught again, her eyes widening in amazement.

The garden might be strewn with palm trees, and vegetation had been hurled across the paths and lawns, but in this lush climate Nature had reclaimed her domain, throwing out vines and foliage to soften the fallen trunks, and vivid blossoms, crimson and white and vermillion pink, to festoon the emerald greenery. And beyond—oh, beyond glistened the brilliance of the azure sea, dazzling in the hot sun. The whole scene was radiant with light and vivid colour.

'It's *fantastic*!' she breathed in wonder.

She could see in an instant why the hotel had been built here, right at the sea's edge, fringed with sand so silver she could barely look at it in the bright sunlight. The contrast with the rank, ruined interior could not have been greater. Talia could feel her spirits lift, her face light up with pleasure at the sight.

'Not bad, is it?' Luke had stepped up beside her. His voice was dry and he was gazing around.

She turned to him. There had been something in his voice, in its very understatedness, that made her exclaim, 'I can see why you want it! It's worth any price!'

His eyes came to rest on her and she could see that for a second, just the barest second, he reeled. But then his gaze shuttered and she could tell that he was deliberately blanking her again.

'I don't get sentimental over projects,' he said tersely. 'That doesn't make me money. What makes me money is buying something at a good price and adding value. That's the opportunity here. The company that owns it wants shot of it, and if I can get it at the right price, and get the refurb costings right, it *will* make me money. That's all I'm interested in.'

How sad, Talia thought. What a shame that this place would be all about money. Where was his heart? Where was his soul? Where was the man she'd spent that incredible night with? The one who had lit up her whole world with his ideas, his passion, his determination?

'Even at the lowest possible cost a refurb will be expensive. More so than a new build because of the clearance costs.'

He glanced at her again. 'Go around the place—and watch your step. Meet me back here in forty-five minutes. Don't keep me waiting.'

He strode off, heading down to the shore, already on his phone.

Talia watched him go, watched his assured, powerful stride carving through the debris in the devastated gardens. There was a heaviness inside her. His blunt words had had a bleak familiarity to them. She knew that attitude, all right. It was her father's. Minimum cost, maximum profit. That was all he'd cared about, too.

It was chilling to see it echoed in Luke.

Then, with a little shake of her head, as if to clear all such thoughts from it, she went back inside and started her tour.

She fished out her notebook from her tote and started to jot things down—rough measurements to begin with, and then a sketchy layout of the ground floor guest areas as she walked, watching her step, through the desolate rooms.

As she did so her mood changed. She wasn't quite plunged automatically into professional mode, but she did find that, despite the desolation and destruction, the same lifting of her spirits was hitting her as when she'd seen the vista of the sea beyond the gardens.

If she looked past the devastation and ruin to the structure of the building she could see that this was, indeed, a beautiful space. With imagination and enthusiasm it could be made impressive again.

Ideas started to flow and her pen moved faster over the paper. She turned pages one after the other, and took copious photos on her phone of rooms and vistas.

She headed upstairs, ideas still pouring through her, a sense of excitement filling her.

For the first time she was being given an opportunity to use her own creativity, to craft her own vision! Being allowed to give her ideas full rein and not have them ignored and dismissed by her father was a liberation.

Time flew by, and only when she saw Luke waiting for her down in the desolate atrium, with a dark expression on his face, did her mood crash again.

'When I say forty-five minutes that is what I mean,' he informed her tightly.

Talia's apology died on her lips.

'I've got some letters to dictate to you,' he continued. 'While you're here you might as well do some secretarial work for me, as well. We'll do it in the car.'

'Er… I don't take dictation,' she said. It wasn't a refusal, only a description of her secretarial limits.

'Tough,' he said.

She stared after him, her heart sinking. His mood was black, that was obvious, and she could only assume it was because the state of the hotel was worse than he'd realised.

As for acting as his secretary, well… She sighed inwardly. If that was what he wanted she would do her best. After all, to have stayed on at the villa paying rent would have cost her a fortune—whatever work she did here for him he was therefore entitled to, even if it wasn't what she was trained for.

So she did the best she could, taking down his dictation as he drove. But not only did the SUV jolting over the potholed roads make it difficult to write, but the complex legalese and financial figures he dictated at high speed tested her meagre abilities to the limit. The fact that she was only exacerbating his bad mood by asking him to slow down or repeat himself was patently visible.

By the time they finally arrived back at the villa there was a headache around her skull like a steel band in full swing.

Luke turned to her. 'There's a government minister I have to see. Those letters need to be typed up this afternoon. There's an office set up in the villa somewhere—the staff will show you.'

Talia nodded dumbly, heading up to her room to shower and change. Was this distant, terse man really the same man as the one she had encountered that fateful evening at the party? How could he be?

She felt her throat catch and hurried into the bathroom. Beneath the flow of water, she was only too conscious of her nakedness—a nakedness she had so briefly gloried in with the man who now looked right through her…

Memories rushed back into her head of when his gaze upon her had not been cold, nor indifferent. But these were memories she did not want and could not afford. She sighed grimly. She couldn't afford much at all.

Enveloping herself tightly in a bath towel, she emerged, steeling herself. What did it matter if Luke now looked right through her and gave her orders and instructions as if nothing had ever happened between them? It would simply remind her of what she shouldn't forget, even for a moment. That she was here for one purpose only—to work as he directed, so that her mother could have some reprieve from the loss of the final piece of her stricken life to which she was still so desperately clinging.

A knock sounded at the door and she went to open it. One of the soft-footed maids came in with a lunch tray, carrying it through to the balcony, on which a little table and chair had been set up under an awning. Talia threw on a sundress, and followed her.

She felt her spirits lift again in the heat and brightness after the dim cool of the air-conditioned bedroom.

Thanking the maid, she felt suddenly hungry and fell to eating. She'd hardly had time for breakfast—which had been served up here in her room—before she'd been informed that

Mr Xenakis was waiting for her, and jet lag had also confused her hunger cues. Now they were fully restored, and she ate with relish the food that had been provided for her: chicken salad, cane juice, and fresh fruit.

As she ate, she gazed out at the vista. And such a vista! Now, for the first time, she could really appreciate where she was.

The villa was set on a slope, high above the sea, which was several miles away across lush countryside, and the beautiful gardens she'd seen from the carriage sweep were wrapped around the back as well.

Was that…? Ah, yes. Her eyes lit up. There was a large turquoise pool, glinting at the rear of the villa. And as she gazed in delighted appreciation she knew, instinctively, that the colour palette for her design ideas was right in front of her: the deep cobalt sea, the turquoise pool, the emerald vegetation, the vivid crimson of the bougainvillea and fragrant frangipani. All would be called upon.

Enthusiasm fired her, and she longed to make a start on her colour boards and sketch out the vision that danced inside her head. Her ideas began to fizz and bubble in her imagination.

But that was not what she'd been instructed

'What's happened to those letters I left you to type up?' he demanded.

'I… I've done them. That's why I thought it would be OK to have a swim,' she said falteringly.

Clumsily, she hurried to get out of the pool, wading up the steps. As she emerged she was burningly conscious that, even though she was wearing a plain one-piece suit, it was clinging to her body, exposing every curve and a lot of bare leg. She seized a towel and wound it round her body while her wet hair streamed water down her back.

His eyes were on her, she could tell, and she felt colour flare out across her cheeks as she dipped her head, squeezing water out of her long hair. She hoped he would go, so she could escape up to her room, but he was not done with her yet.

'My PA said she's received nothing,' he retorted.

She looked confused. 'You didn't say anything about sending them anywhere. And I don't have any contact details.'

He cut across her. 'It will have to be done *now*.' His mouth tightened. 'Get changed and meet me in the office.'

He strode off before she could make any reply, and disappeared indoors. Hurriedly,

to do this afternoon. There were Luke's letters to type up first.

The office she was shown into by the stately butler—whose name, he informed her upon enquiry, was Fernando—was chilled with air-conditioning and had no outside light coming in. The windows were high set, with venetian blinds over them. An array of high-tech equipment hummed to one side, and a huge PC sat on the desk.

She took her place in front of it and got out her notebook. She sighed, hoping she would be able to decipher what she'd scrawled so hectically.

It proved hard going, and she knew, with a sinking heart, that she was making a poor fist of it. She did her best, all the same, though she was painstakingly slow, not being able to touch-type, and found the keyboard complicated to operate when it came to tabulating the many figures Luke had thrown at her.

Finally, she was done, though there were gaps and queries in every letter and attachment. She could only hope that Luke would make allowances for the fact that she was not a trained secretary and they had been going over a bumpy road while she was trying to write it all down.

The headache, which had cleared over lunch

in the fresh air, was now back with a vengeance. With a final sigh of abject relief, she closed down the word processing software and got up, her back stiff and sore from hours of hunching over the keyboard.

Then her face brightened.

The pool! She would freshen up with a dip—that, surely, would clear her head and loosen her stiff limbs. And she would ask the Fernando if she could have a coffee, and a long juice drink.

A handful of minutes later she was plunging head-first into blissfully warm water, joyfully dipping her head under the water to feel her hair stream wetly down her back. Her spirits soared. Oh, this was joyous! She splashed around, frolicking like a child, delighting in the diamond sprays of water catching the late-afternoon sunshine, then pushed off the side, plunging in a duck-dive to the tiled bottom of the pool, dappled with sunlight. Then:

'What the *hell* do you think you're doing?'

CHAPTER FIVE

THE STENTORIAN VOICE halted Talia mid-plunge and she floundered back up. Her eyes went to the edge of the pool as she brushed the strands of wet hair from her face.

Luke was standing there, glowering down at her. Talia blenched, grabbing the edge of the pool to steady herself. 'I… I wanted a swim,' she said.

She didn't try to make her voice sound defiant—let alone entitled—but Luke seemed to take it that way. She could tell by the instant darkening of his eyes.

'May I remind you,' he bit out, and the sarcasm was blatant in his clipped words, 'that you are here to work. This is *not* a holiday for you!'

She saw him breathe in sharply, lips pressing in a thin line.

Talia opened her mouth to tell him she knew that, and understood it only too clearly, but he forestalled her attempt at self-defence.

Talia ran up to her room. The bad mood that had encompassed him as they'd left the hotel was clearly still clinging to him, and when she joined him again, as quickly as she could, she saw with a sinking heart that it had only worsened.

He was sitting at the computer, her work on the screen. At her entry he turned. 'This,' he said grimly, 'is a complete mess.'

He lifted a hand to indicate the screen, where one of his long, complicated letters was displayed. There were half-sentences in red, to show where she wasn't sure she'd taken down what he'd said correctly, and there were queries and question marks freely dispersed throughout.

Talia pressed her hands together. 'I told you,' she said, her voice as composed as she could make it—which was not very much, 'I don't take dictation and it was hard to write in the car because of the bumpy road. You gave me very little time, and these letters deal with matters I'm not familiar with.' She swallowed. 'I did my best,' she said.

She could feel her throat constricting and sense tears building up behind her eyelashes. She was reminded of how once, when she was a novice designer, her father had given her instructions she hadn't been able to carry out. His anger had wiped the floor with her. She had cried, and he had been even angrier. But she wouldn't cry in front of Luke—she wouldn't!

Gritting her teeth, she blinked rapidly, taking the seat that Luke was now vacating with a bowed head. He positioned himself behind her, so he could read the screen as well, and she felt the closeness of his presence overpowering her.

'OK,' he said tersely. 'I'll give you the corrections.'

He did so, and her fingers stumbled on the keyboard, but she soldiered on, blinking away the haze in her eyes as she laboured over the intricate figures, the complicated tabulation they required, and then added headings for addresses and pagination as well.

It seemed to take for ever, and her head was aching again with the concentration and fumbling finger-work, but finally it seemed he was done. Done with the work and done with her. She hit 'send' on the set of documents, to the email address he'd dictated, and sat back, her hands falling nervously to her lap.

Behind her, Luke spoke in that remote, impersonal tone she was getting used to.

'You can clock off now. And you can have the evening to yourself—I'm dining out. Tomorrow, make a start on your initial design ideas. As for any more secretarial work...' his voice tightened. 'I'll use an agency.'

He walked out and, feeling crushed yet again, Talia slowly made her way upstairs to the sanctuary of her bedroom, lying for a long while flat on the bed, staring blankly at the ceiling.

The man she had once known so briefly, so incandescently, who had for a short few hours transformed the world for her, who had looked on her with passion and desire, had gone. Gone for ever.

A bleakness filled her. A sense of desolation. She felt her eyes haze over again, and this time she did not try and suppress her tears... her hopeless, flowing tears...

Luke was having dinner with one of the senior civil servants in the Department of Business Development, but he scarcely heard what the man was saying. His thoughts were elsewhere, circling round and round in his head like a vulture, and he could not banish them.

I can do this. I can do it and I will do it. I must. I will make myself immune to her and I absolutely will succeed!

But it was proving harder than he'd thought—damnably harder! Being with her again, tormented by all the memories of their unforgettable encounter, he'd felt his eyes constantly wanting to go to her, to drink her in.

It was bad enough when she was looking the way she had on the flight, or at dinner last night, and on the drive to the hotel site—so withdrawn and expressionless. But then—he felt emotion stab at him—at the hotel, when she'd walked out into the garden, her face and her eyes had come alive with delight and pleasure. The radiance in her expression! That brief moment of shared feeling with her.

He'd had to force himself to be terse, to stamp down on her enthusiasm, ramming home to her the fact that he was only interested in the profit he could make—that he did not get sentimental over projects.

Or sentimental about her, *either.*

That was the message he had to convey. His jaw tensed in recollection. And it was the only message he had allowed himself to convey when he'd come across her cavorting in the pool that afternoon. Harsh displeasure. Because if he hadn't—

I couldn't have coped with seeing her glorious figure, so nearly naked, that swimsuit clinging to her lush curves and slim waist.

So he'd made himself speak angrily to her—

but the anger had been for himself, at his own weakness. His own vulnerability to her.

His hands tightened on his knife and fork as he made some abstracted reply to whatever had been said to him.

I will not be vulnerable to her—not again. Never again. I will not let myself desire her, or want her, or crave her. I brought her here only to teach myself how to be immune to her. How to feel indifferent as well as to pretend indifference. And I will succeed. I must succeed.

His host was speaking again, asking him about his plans, and he forced himself to focus. There was no point replaying the day in his head...no point letting his thoughts go to the villa, where Talia would be dining alone, going to bed alone...

He reached for his wine and knocked it back. He wanted to gain some strength from it but all he felt was tempted. Unbearably tempted by Talia...

Talia settled herself down at the table that Fernando and his staff had carried out onto her wide balcony, underneath a shady awning. A light breeze sifted off the sea far below, lifting the heat, and the awning took the blaze of the sun off her. Down in the gardens she could hear birdsong, and occasionally the voices of the villa's staff as they went about their work.

It was very peaceful.

It was a peace she was trying to find inside her own head—hard though it was. She had slept restlessly, neither comfortable with the air-conditioning nor without it, and had stepped out at one point onto the dark balcony to be enveloped in the balmy warmth of the night, to hear the incessant chirruping of the tree frogs all around her. The moon had sailed overhead and she'd felt her lungs tighten; she'd heard her mother's voice again, unbidden, talking about the joy of being romanced beneath a tropical moon…

She'd gone back indoors, the words ringing hollow in her head. Luke had returned quite late—she'd heard the car—and had, it seemed, retired immediately. She'd been in her bedroom, where the staff had served dinner—delicious, but lonely—after which she'd spent some time emailing her mother, doing her best to sound cheerful.

She'd told her mum about the site visit, the ideas she had come up with, and how excited she was about them; she'd explained that she would be working on them tomorrow, described the beautiful island, the hot weather, and reassured her that the jet lag was easing.

But that was all that was easing, because this morning had brought no sign of any thaw from Luke. She hadn't even set eyes on him. Breakfast had been served in her room, and when she had asked after Luke, somewhat tentatively, she had been informed that he would be out all day and he had instructed her to work from the villa.

So now she began to develop her ideas for the hotel refurbishment, reaching for her art paper, her paints and pencils. She got out her notebook with the rough floor plans and measurements, and loaded the copious photos she'd taken the day before onto her laptop.

As she scrolled through them she began to feel the same emotions building up in her that she had felt on site and at lunchtime yesterday. Enthusiasm started to fire in her. The hotel was in such a beautiful situation, its architecture so perfect for its shoreline position between the azure ocean and the emerald rainforest, how could she fail to want to see it restored to beauty? To rescue it from the decay and ruin it had been subjected to?

I'll make it beautiful again. I'll make it more beautiful than ever.

A thought ran through her head—one she clutched at. She would do it for Luke. For the man with whom she had spent that magical night. Not the man who was now treating her with such callous indifference.

He no longer wanted her, and was making it glaringly obvious that whatever had burned so brightly and yet so briefly between them was nothing more than dead ashes now, but still she would use whatever talent she possessed to show him how beautiful that sad, ruined place of devastation could be.

If her design talents were all he wanted of her now, those at least he would have.

With renewed determination, she got to work.

Luke strode back into the villa. He'd had a long day. Frustration was biting at him. He'd met with another bunch of civil servants and the site's owners in the morning—relatives, he knew, of the government Minister for Development—and the message he was getting from them was loud and clear. They wanted him to buy the site—but at a price he was in no way prepared to pay.

Meetings in the afternoon with the architect and the structural engineering firm he intended to use had indicated that the cost of restoration was going to be astronomical, and then he'd made another lengthy visit to the hotel.

He flexed his shoulders as he headed into

the office to communicate with his PA in Lucerne. It was time for some tough negotiations to commence.

He relished the prospect.

What he did not relish was what he was about to do.

He settled himself at the desk and picked up the house phone. 'Fernando, please inform Ms Grantham that I require her company this evening. Tell her to be ready for six thirty—formal evening wear. It is a reception at the Minister for Development's residence, with dinner afterwards.'

He set down the phone, his expression flickering. Should he really do this? Should he really spend the evening with her? But how else was he going to make himself immune to her except by spending time with her? It had to be done.

I can do it. I will do it. I must do it.

It was a mantra he repeated to himself that evening, as they took their seats in the back of the chauffeured car that set off from the villa.

He'd said nothing to Talia as she'd joined him in the hall on the dot of half past six, just given her a brief nod of acknowledgement before heading out to the car. Now, as she sat beside him, assiduously looking out of the window instead of at him, he allowed himself a glance at her. Then he forced himself to really look at her. Forced himself to take in her profile and the soft swell of her breast, to catch the fragrance she was wearing. He *made* his senses endure it.

When they arrived, some twenty minutes later, at the lavish private residence of the government minister, they walked into the crowded interior past flambeaux flaring beside the portico. He did not offer Talia his arm—that was something he knew he could not endure—but he did endure the minister who, on seeing him arrive, strolled up to them with a genial smile on his face. He greeted Luke and clearly expected an introduction to the woman at his side.

'My...secretary,' Luke heard himself say.

What he'd intended by saying that was not to let the minister know that he was already progressing to interior design for the hotel. For that would reveal the extent of his interest in the purchase, thus weakening his bargaining position. But too late he realised that the note of hesitation in his description of Talia's role was fuelling an appreciative look from the minister, who was drawing a quite different conclusion.

'I wish *my* secretary were as beautiful as

you, my dear.' The minister smiled at Talia, his gaze openly admiring.

Luke felt his hand clench. A primitive urge speared him—a desire to whisk Talia away from any man who cast such a look at her. And an even more primitive urge pierced him when he heard Talia give a light laugh at the compliment.

Then the minister was greeting another new arrival and Luke promptly clamped a hand over Talia's elbow, steering her away. He felt her wince at the tightness of his grip and let her go. A waiter glided up to them, bearing a drinks tray, and Luke took two glasses, handed one to Talia.

'I need to network,' he said. And then, before he could stop himself, he heard words fall from his lips which he instantly regretted but could not prevent, because of the dark thorn of jealousy that was driving him. 'Try *not* to flirt with every man here.'

He heard a low gasp from Talia but ignored it, moving forward to greet one of the minister's aides whom he'd met that afternoon.

Talia's lips pressed together. There had been no call for him to say such a thing to her.

What does he think I should have done? Told the minister whose approval he needs for

*his project that my looks have nothing to do
with my professional competence?*

She'd got through the moment in as graceful
a fashion as she could, having had long experience of such comments and heavy-handed
admiration in her years of endless hateful socialising at her father's side.

Feeling awkward in the extreme—as she
had from the moment she'd climbed into the
car beside Luke, with the atmosphere between
them more distant than ever—all she could do
now was fall automatically into the routine
that she was familiar with at functions like
this: murmuring anodyne greetings, keeping
quietly at Luke's side as she had at her father's.

Her father had required her to be merely
ornamental. Was that why Luke had brought
her here?

Her mouth thinned painfully. It certainly
was not for the pleasure of her company, that
was for sure! She was punishingly aware, and
it made her feel horribly constrained herself,
that he'd not spoken a word to her except that
totally unfair comment just now, which had
stung her to the quick. And he was broadcast-
ing on every frequency the fact that he had
no interest whatsoever in her being with him.

So why had he stipulated that he required
her presence?

As she did what was presumably her duty at his side—being his 'plus one' for the evening—it started to dawn on her why he might have insisted she come with him tonight.

Did he want to keep other women at bay? Was that it? Because it was clear, now that she paid attention to it, that he was being eyed up—covertly *and* not so covertly—by female eyes all around. Her mouth thinned painfully again. She couldn't blame them for gazing at him. *All* women would take one look and crave him.

The way I do.

She pushed the bleak, hopeless thought out of her head, letting the familiar anguish fill her instead. She had had her chance with Luke and had walked out on it. Although it had been for reasons way beyond her control at the time, the result had been the same—she had left when she had desperately wanted to stay, and her lack of courage in that moment had spoiled everything.

He doesn't want me any more. There's nothing left of what there was. Nothing at all...

She sighed. All that was between them now was the fact that, for some reason she really didn't understand, he had brought her here to do a job. She must be grateful for that. Grateful that he'd heard her plea not to be evicted from the Marbella villa immediately. Grateful for the generous terms he'd offered. And that generosity was undeniable, she knew. What she would have been paid for her interior design skills wasn't even close to three months' market rate rent on the villa.

No wonder he wanted her to do every extra he cared to chuck at her, she thought bitterly. From being his secretary—however useless he thought her—to accompanying him to glitzy networking events like this, the purpose of which, she could only suppose, was to shield him from a horde of eager females waiting for their opportunity to pounce.

He seemed to be making methodical progress around the room, selecting various individuals to talk to, and from his conversation it was clear to Talia that for him this was simply an extended business meeting. She didn't follow most of it, confining herself to shadowing him meekly and being mindful not to 'flirt'— as he had so sneeringly and so unfairly put it. She stayed as modest and docile as she could, while trying not to appear dull or boring.

It was more of a skill than she knew Luke would credit, and it had been learned from years beside her father.

The thought was bleak, bringing home to

her just how little she meant to Luke. Less than little.

'Right, we can leave now.'

His voice interrupted her painful cogitations. She felt her elbow gripped again—in that tight, commanding hold that steered her purposefully in any direction he wanted. They were soon crossing the large room, pausing only for Luke to shake hands several times and make his farewells as they left. Dutifully, Talia, too, murmured her goodbyes, bestowed civil smiles, and then, finally, they were outside in the warm night air, before the chill of the air-conditioned car enveloped her.

Luke threw himself in beside her, leaning forward to instruct the driver.

Talia heard him give the name of the island's most famous hotel.

Now what?

It was dinner. As docilely as she had at the minister's cocktail party, Talia walked in beside Luke, the skirts of her evening gown swishing around her legs. She was grateful she'd packed it, having not been sure just what she should bring with her. It was a world away, she thought with a pang, from the tightly sheathing dark red dress she'd worn at the party where she'd met Luke. This, like all her evening gowns, had been chosen to suit her father's taste—fussier and more embellished than she would have liked. But her father had wanted her to look expensive, to show the world how wealthy he was.

Her eyes shadowed. That life had gone for ever, and now she was picking her way across the bomb site that was all she and her mother had left. She was trying to protect her mother as best she could, whatever it took. Including being here like this with Luke.

It was a mockery—oh, *such* a mockery—of the way they'd been that magical evening at the party! The coldness of his manner burned her, as if she'd swallowed bitter acid.

With that sourness in her throat, she took her seat at the table reserved for them, quietly accepted the menu and started to peruse it. Why had Luke brought her here? If her role as minder—keeping females from pestering him—was no longer necessary, he could easily have sent her back to the villa. But, whatever his purpose in bringing her here, she just had to cope with it, however painful.

She stole a glance at him. He was absorbed in the menu, and then the wine list, his expression closed. The waiter came to pour water, bestow a basket of rolls upon the table, and then he stood and waited for their orders. She gave hers, smiling up at the young waiter,

JULIA JAMES 113

whose face split into a wide, answering smile as he repeated her order in his lilting Caribbean accent. She heard Luke give his order in the terse tone that was becoming grimly familiar to Talia. Then the waiter nodded and headed off.

'Try not to flirt with the waiting staff, either.'

Talia's snapped her head towards Luke, eyes widening. 'I *wasn't*!' she said, breathless with indignation.

'He couldn't take his eyes off you,' came his reply. His eyes narrowed. 'No man can.'

He glanced towards another table nearby, where two men were openly casting their eyes in Talia's direction. He couldn't blame them. Even in that unflattering evening gown of hers she was the most beautiful woman in the room. His jaw tightened, and he felt the scythe of emotion scissoring within him yet again. She'd been the most beautiful woman at the cocktail party and she was the most beautiful woman here.

The most beautiful woman anywhere she goes...

His eyes swept back to her. She'd dipped her head at his words, that wash of colour he'd seen before when he'd spoken sharply to her flushing across her sculpted cheeks.

It made him angry. But it was an anger that came from deep within. An anger that was *in* himself—*at* himself. He could feel his gaze drinking her in, absorbing the way the long lashes of her tawny eyes dusted the delicate curve of her cheek, how her rich mouth trembled, how the sweep of her hair exposed the graceful line of her throat…

Desire flooded him. Longing…

He cut it off, refusing to acknowledge it. He told himself yet again that the only reason he had brought her with him tonight was to inure himself to her, and that he must succeed in doing so.

To stop himself looking at her again, he beckoned the sommelier to the table, immersing himself in a discussion of wines. Yet he was still burningly conscious that across the table from him Talia's slender fingers were pulling a soft roll to pieces. Her head was still dipped, her eyes averted from him.

He chose the requisite wine, busied himself with its tasting and approval, then dismissed the sommelier and turned his attention back to Talia. He wanted to find something in her to criticise, something to bolster his determination to make himself immune to her.

His eyes alighted on her gown. He frowned. It really did nothing to accentuate her stunning beauty—and, whilst he knew he should be pleased, he heard himself say, his tone critical, 'Is that dress by the same designer as the dress you wore at the villa?'

She started, as if she hadn't expected him to talk to her. 'Er…yes,' she answered. Her expression was wary.

'It doesn't suit you,' he said bluntly. His eyes flicked over her dismissively, and he saw that flush of colour run out over her cheeks again. 'It's far too fussy and over-embellished.' Before he could stop himself, he added, 'Nothing like what you were wearing at that party—'

As the words left his lips he cursed himself. The last thing he needed to do was remind himself of that night.

But Talia was only dipping her head again, saying in a pinched voice, 'My father liked this kind of style. He said it was very feminine. It was the way he liked me to look.'

Luke's expression tightened. So she'd dressed to please her doting father? That shouldn't surprise him—after all, it was Gerald Grantham who'd bankrolled her luxury lifestyle.

Abruptly, he changed the subject. He shouldn't give a damn *what* her dress was like—the less flattering to her the better, as far as he was concerned!

'So, what progress have you made on your design ideas?' he put to her as their first course arrived.

She lifted her head again and took a steadying breath. 'I'm working on a colour palette at the moment. You told me to come up with my own ideas, but if you want me to run them past you, in case you don't like them—' she started.

He cut across her. 'When I hire professionals I don't expect to have to do their job for them,' he said brusquely.

She flushed, yet again, and said falteringly, 'That isn't what I meant. I just thought that if I'm coming up with some ideas you dislike from the off you might as well tell me now, so I can make it how you want.'

He took a draught from his wine glass. 'If I don't like them I won't use them,' he said. He set his glass back on the table. 'Tell me, what kind of commercial experience do you have? Anything I might have come across?'

She took a breath. 'I did all the interiors of my father's properties, but—'

She was going to say, *But please don't judge me on that work. I had to stick to my father's exacting brief, not use my own ideas.*

She never got a chance to finish. A frown

had flashed across Luke's face, drawing his brows together darkly.

'You never told me that.'

He made it sound like an accusation, and Talia felt herself flushing. 'You've never asked me anything about what I've done,' she started to protest in her own defence, wanting to let him know that the work she'd done for her father did *not* represent her creative skills.

But Luke was already speaking again, his frown deepening. 'What have you done for other clients?' he demanded.

She felt herself hesitating, but answered truthfully. 'Um…nothing. But—'

She tried to get out the fact that her father had not permitted her to work for anyone else but, as before, Luke cut right across her, his frown deeper again.

'Are you telling me that *all* your work has been for your father?'

The scathing note in his voice was unmistakable and Talia winced inwardly, knowing that if he'd seen any of the garish interiors she'd done for her father he would judge her by them—critically.

'Well?' Luke demanded, clearly wanting an answer.

She swallowed, nodding, and again tried to explain just why that was, and that the work did not represent what she was capable of stylistically. But Luke gave her no chance.

She heard him mutter something under his breath in Greek. It sounded disparaging, even though she hadn't a clue what it meant. Then he was eyeballing her again, his jaw set. Pointedly, he threw another question at her.

'So, what do you make of this place, then? From a professional point of view,' he asked her. His voice was sharp suddenly, his gaze pinning her. Challenging her.

She glanced around the opulent dining room, trying to gather her thoughts in what was becoming his blatant interrogation—and a hostile one at that. She felt wrong-footed, and tried to recover her composure.

'It's very…impressive,' she said.

She chose the word carefully. Personally, she thought the opulent gilded furnishings and décor out of place on a tropical island, but she did not wish to insult the famous designer whose hallmark was evident here.

Luke's eyes narrowed. 'And will you be attempting to emulate this style yourself?'

She looked at him uncertainly. His question had sounded sardonic, and she wasn't sure why.

'I would do my best, if that was what you wanted,' she replied neutrally.

It was the last thing she would choose her-self—to impose this kind of overblown style on that devastated, hurricane-blasted hotel. It would be totally wrong for it.

She never got the chance to say so. He was nodding, his expression hardening. 'Ah, yes—just as you "did your best" typing up those let-ters so atrociously!'

She flushed at the derision in his voice. To her dismay, as when he'd been correcting her hopeless typing, pushing her harder and harder, she felt tears haze her eyes. She felt her throat tightening and tried to fight it in vain, blinking rapidly to try and clear the treacher-ous mist that was forming.

Unhappiness twisted inside her. Why was he getting at her over this? Why was he jab-bing at her with everything he said? She dipped her head, taking another mouthful of her food, though it suddenly tasted like ashes in her mouth.

Luke's expression tightened. The revelation she'd made that the only design experience she actually had was courtesy of her father was damning. Totally damning! She obviously wasn't a professional interior designer in the least. She was nothing but a dabbling ama-teur—a rich man's daughter who'd clearly fancied the idea of interior design as something to while away the time between shopping and socialising.

Her doting father had indulged her and she had amused herself by producing interiors that were, without exception, in every property belonging to Grantham Land that he had seen since his acquisition, uniformly hideous! Flashy, ostentatious, and tasteless.

Luke's expression tightened even more. There wasn't a chance in hell she could come up with something that was of the slightest use to him.

But do I actually want to use anything she might produce anyway?

Would he really want anything to remind himself of her in his new hotel?

His eyes rested on her again as he faced up to the realisation. She'd dipped her head again, was mechanically eating her food, yet he could see that her expression was pinched. It irritated him. He didn't want her looking like that—looking as if he'd hurt her feelings by what he'd said to her. What he *wanted*, damn it, was to feel nothing about her at all!

But he wasn't succeeding, he wasn't succeeding at all.

'Talia—' Was his voice harsh? He didn't mean it to be, but it had come out that way.

Her head shot up and he saw, with that same spike of emotion that had made him not want to see her looking upset, that the pinched look was more pronounced than ever, that her lower lip was trembling, that there was a liquid haze over her eyes…

He dropped an oath in Greek. He was impatient. Angry. Angry at what he was fighting to crush back inside him.

'Don't try and make me feel sorry for you to get yourself an easier ride.' He was proud that his voice had come out flat rather than cutting. 'I offered you this job in good faith—and on extremely generous terms! The fact that you have financial woes is not my problem—so don't ask for any sympathy from me on that score.'

He wouldn't forget the hell her father had put his family through, or how he had watched them suffer before they died. Talia had lived like a pampered princess, while his own father had—

There was a sudden clatter as she dropped her knife and fork on her plate. He saw her expression change. Change totally. Suddenly she was angry, and her voice bit out as she cut across him.

'I am *not* asking for sympathy!' Her eyes flashed furiously. 'I am extremely grateful for your commission, and I am more than willing to do any ancillary work for that you may require. But I am *not* going to apologise for my failings as a secretary when I simply do not have the skills or training!'

She took a heaving breath, an audible intake, before plunging on, even more furiously.

'Nor is there *any* justification for you biting my head off every time I speak! And as for my behaviour—' her eyes flashed again '—I will *not* be subjected to your totally unwarranted accusations that I am flirting with *anyone*! You have absolutely *no* right to make *any* comments of that nature whatsoever. And if you can't tell the difference between civility and sexual come-ons, then that is *your* problem, not *mine*!'

Talia pushed her chair back, getting to her feet. Emotion was ripping her apart and she didn't care. She didn't care what she was saying or what the consequences would be. She had *had* it with the man! She wasn't going to take one more jibe, one more put-down! Not *one*!

'It is not part of my professional engagement to spend my evenings with you—and this one is terminating right *now*!'

Tossing her napkin onto her chair, she turned on her heel, striding across the wide dining room, a red mist in her vision. She had *had* it with the jibes, the accusations—the whole damn lot!

Emotion raged within her as she strode out into the hotel lobby. Anger was uppermost—she had been pushed beyond what any person could endure—but there was so much more in her than anger.

She felt her chest tighten like a drum and her throat constrict. There was a haze in front of her vision, as well as the red mist of rage. She wanted out—oh, dear God, she wanted out! And not just out of this overdone hotel that screamed *Money! Money! Money! Money!* in her face with every piece of over-decorated gilded furniture and cream satin fabric and every ludicrously over-the-top floral arrangement on every available marble surface.

She wanted *out* of this unbearable situation. To be so close to Luke and yet as distant from him as the stars was torture. And for him to be doing nothing but taking pot-shots at her, criticising her and berating her so that she could do nothing right—nothing at all… It was as if he were a completely different person from the one she'd thought she'd known—as if that rapturous night she'd spent with him, when she'd had to tear herself away from him with all the strength in her body and soul, had never happened!

To think she had so stupidly, so pathetically hoped that maybe she would have a second chance with him to make up for having had to run out on him the way she had. What a fool to think they could recover the bliss they had found so briefly.

Misery consumed her, thick and choking in her lungs, as dense as the hot, humid air that hit her as she rushed out onto the forecourt. Blindly, she threw herself into the first taxi waiting there, summoned by a doorman who had hastened to open the door for her as she stumbled inside.

The taxi pulled off and she slumped back, numb to everything except an all-consuming misery.

CHAPTER SIX

LUKE JERKED HIS chair back, watching her rush from the dining room. For a moment he was simply frozen. Then, vaulting upright, he started after her.

But suddenly the maître d' was there, consternation on his face, expressing his concern, asking if everything was all right, if there was something wrong with the food, the wine, the service, the staff—

'No, nothing!' Luke exclaimed, wanting only to push past the man and catch up with Talia, who was disappearing across the lobby, heading for the huge glass doors beyond. 'My apologies!' he threw at the maître d', finally getting past him.

Then, in the lobby, he was delayed again, by a party arriving at the hotel who were filling up the entrance. By the time he emerged out onto the forecourt she was gone.

'Get my car!' he snapped at the doorman,

who promptly got on his phone to the chauffeurs' station.

It seemed to take an age for the limo to appear. He couldn't complain—his driver would hardly have thought he would be leaving so soon after arriving.

He sank into the back of the car, cutting short the driver's apologies for the delay. 'It doesn't matter. Just get me back to the villa ASAP!'

Urgency possessed him. Urgency and a whole lot more.

Never had a car journey seemed longer, or more tormenting.

Never had emotion burned him to the quick like this, crying out the lie he was trying to cling to—the lie that was impossible to fool himself into believing any longer.

I can never be indifferent to her. I will never be immune to her.

The very words mocked him pitilessly, rendering to ashes all he had felt, all he had believed, since the woman with whom he had shared a life-changing night had left him with barely a word.

Talia clattered up the wide staircase, ignoring Fernando's stately greeting and his enquiry if there was anything she wanted.

Yes, to get out of here! Just get out! To get to the airport and on the first flight home.

But how could she? And where was 'home' now?

If she wanted to keep her poor stricken mother, so utterly unable to cope with the catastrophe that had torn her life apart, somewhere familiar and comfortable while she built up her strength, then she must stick this out. She had to go on enduring the torment of Luke being so horrible, so different from the man she'd spent that night with.

She was trapped here—hideously, unbearably trapped. Perhaps he would not even keep to their deal after her outburst in the restaurant.

Tears were choking her as she reached her bedroom, leaning back against the door in anguish, features contorted, consumed by the misery that encompassed her. She kicked off her shoes, struggled out of her evening gown, her underwear, and enveloped herself in her kimono-style robe. Finally she collapsed down onto the dressing table stool and frantically unpinned her hair. She brushed it with harsh, painful strokes, as if she could brush out far more than the knots that tangled it.

Emotions raged within her, hot and heavy and choking, and she batted away the pointless tears. This wasn't Luke! Not the man she'd known—the man she'd found such incandescent, incredible bliss with. The man who had taken her to a paradise she had never known existed. The man who had wanted to whisk her away from the misery of her life, to sweep her off in his arms to a tropical island, to a place that could be theirs and theirs alone.

The choking came in her throat again, suffocating her with anguish. A cry rose within her. Oh, dear God, the bitter irony of it. For she *was* here on a tropical island with him. One of the thousand islands in the Caribbean that they might have run away to…

Her face contorted with anguish again. Oh, she was here on a beautiful, sun-kissed Caribbean island, all right—but not with Luke. Or at least not with the man she had thought he was. She was here with a hard-faced, cruel-voiced stranger who only found fault with her. A petty tyrant like her father, carping and dismissive.

Not Luke. It wasn't Luke at all.

That man I knew so briefly, so wonderfully, is gone. Gone and never coming back. Or perhaps that was never the man he truly is in the first place. Perhaps this Luke is the real him.

A sob broke from her, but she stifled it, filled with the misery that had possessed her ever since she had realised that *he* was the man who had brought her father to ruin and then helped himself to the remnants of his business.

In any case, he was supremely indifferent to her now.

It's as though he hates me!

Emotion blasted her once more.

And I hate him. I hate him for the way he is now. I hate him for his indifference, for his coldness, his anger, for his cruelty.

There was a sudden noise behind her. Her bedroom door was flung open and she saw the reason for her devastation reflected in the dressing table mirror.

She whirled around. 'Get out!'

She yelled it with all her strength but Luke did not obey. He strode up to her, dark purpose in his face.

With a smothered gasp of shock Talia lurched to her feet—and then he was in front of her. His eyes blazed with dark light while his hands reached for her, clamping around her upper arms. Heat burned through the thin silk of her sleeve. She reeled with the sensation of it—with his closeness. She could catch the scent of his aftershave, the scent of his body. Her senses were fully awake now, memories buffeting her like the wind on a tiny sailboat in the middle of a stormy sea.

She could not bear it. Could not endure it.

She yelled at him again. Her heart had started to pound, blood was surging in her veins. 'Let go of me! You've got no right! No right to barge in here and manhandle me! So get out—get *out*!'

There was fury in her voice. And desperation. How could he stride in here, looking the way he did? Tall, dark, and so, so dangerous.

He did not let her go. His face twisted, that dark light still blazing in his eyes, and it made her reel with the force of it. She felt faint at the intensity, and suddenly weak with what she dared not face.

She felt herself sway, and only the grip of his steel hands around her arms stayed her.

'Throw me out if you want…' The hoarseness in his voice made it low, like a growl, and it was filled with the same burning intensity that was in his eyes, pouring into hers. 'But not yet. *Not yet.*'

For one endless moment more his dark gaze burned into hers. And then he hauled her to him, his mouth swooping to hers.

The room disappeared. The world disappeared. Everything disappeared. She drowned in his kiss. It was unbearable to kiss him and unthinkable not to. Her hands flashed to his shoulders, grasping them tightly. Then, as suddenly as he had seized her, he relinquished her. He stepped back and gave a harsh, brief laugh that had no humour in it.

His eyes were still blazing down at her. She stared at him, breathless, heart pounding, mouth stung and pouting, stared at the naked passion in his kiss, lips parting helplessly, eyes aching.

'Do you see now why I've been so cruel to you? I've been trying to hold you at bay. I *had* to push you away...' The hoarseness was still in his voice. 'Because it was the only way— the only way to stop myself kissing you like that. It was my only protection.'

His hands fell away from her and she swayed in their absence. Blood was pounding in her ears and racing in her veins. She was dazed.

He gave that harsh, humourless laugh again. 'Tell me to go.' His voice had changed; his stance had changed. The darkness in his eyes had changed. 'Or tell me to stay...'

She could not move, could not speak. She could only stand there, knowing with a kind of fatal awareness that desire had leapt in her body as a kindled flame. That she could feel her breasts filling, peaking, heat flushing up inside her. They were all but declaring her answer to him.

His expression had changed, too, and what was in it now made Talia feel faint again, weak. She could not drag her eyes from him, could not move. She heard him speak again through the blood soaring in her veins.

'You see…' he said softly, and a taunt was there in his voice. But it was not directed at her, she knew, but at himself. 'You see how much protection from you I need.'

He reached a hand towards her as she stood there, so faint, so motionless. He drew one long finger down the length of her cheek, then let it fall away. It was the same casual gesture he had made when he had first touched her on that fateful evening.

She saw his eyes half close, long lashes dipping. She saw the planes of his face, the roughened edge of his jaw, the strong column of his throat, the sable feathering of his hair. She caught again his scent in her nostrils and felt weakness drain through her. This was insanity…madness. It could only be that, surely, after all that had passed between them? To let this happen all over again?

'I want you. I want you as much as I ever did from that very first moment I set eyes on you. It's that simple, Talia. So very, very simple.'

His mouth lowered to hers again, but this

was no demanding kiss, no leap of hot, instant passion. This was slow and sensual and quite, quite deliberate, and it was meant to make her yield to him, to make it impossible for her to hear what every ounce of fading sense was telling her: that this was madness and insanity and she should put a stop to it immediately.

How could she resist? How could she pull away from that honeyed feathering of her lips by his? From the continued arousal of her senses and the blood pounding in her ears? She revelled in the deepening of his kiss as he opened her mouth to him, to taste the sweetness within...

She felt his hands splay around her waist, drawing her pliant form towards the strong pillar of his body. She felt the edges of her robe brush the smooth fabric of his tuxedo jacket, felt the delicate peaks of her breasts unfurl at the frisson, felt her blood bubble and fizz, her desire thicken. Of their own volition her hands lifted to his torso, sliding inside his jacket, feeling, with a leap of her senses, the hard-muscled wall of his chest beneath her fingers.

Her kiss intensified with his and she felt him quicken, the hands at her waist moulding her against him so that her hips were crushed against his. With a smothered gasp, though it should have come as no surprise, she realised his arousal was full and strong. It fed hers— sent heat flushing her core, sent her fingertips into spasm, as her mouth feasted on his and his on hers.

She moaned low in her throat and it was like a match to dry tinder.

He swept her up into his arms, strode to the bed, and lowered her down upon it. He shed his jacket, impatience in every gesture.

She lay there, her blood pounding and leaping in her veins. Desire surged in her limbs, flooding her in hot, hungry urgency. Oh, this was madness, insanity, but she didn't care. Could not care. She could only reach up her arms with a low laugh of delight, of wonder and glory.

This was happening. He was here again— with her—and he was all she wanted.

All she could ever want.

Everything else in the world fell away from her.

There was only Luke. Only his possession of her.

Only that...

The dim light of dawn was filtering through the louvered shutters. Luke lay, sated, with

Talia's soft, silken body in his arms. Idly, he curled a lock of her lush hair around his finger. She was half asleep, her rounded breasts crushed against his chest, her legs tangled with his. Warmth enfolded them both.

At some point in the night he'd turned off the air-conditioning, turned off the light over the dressing table, and let the warm tropical night embrace them as they lay in the wide bed.

A sense of rightness filled him. It was *right* that he had yielded, after all, to what he had been fighting so desperately, so uselessly...

He'd known it the instant she'd stormed away from him in the hotel restaurant. He'd known there was only one thing he wanted— only one thing he could do. And it was what he had wanted from the moment she'd walked into his office in Switzerland—what he had been denying himself.

He'd tried to steel himself against her by any means he could—he'd spoken to her harshly, treated her so distantly, so critically, and he'd tried for indifference with every ounce of his willpower. But his need for her had only grown, and he'd been able to maintain that impossible effort no longer.

He'd had to yield to what he had had wanted every minute of the day and the night.

To possess her again. To make her *his* once more.

After the night they had spent together, the passion that had blazed between them, there was nothing else but what was between them. His finger released the silken tendril and drifted to the silk of her skin instead. He grazed it lightly along the line of her shoulder and felt her quiver at his touch, even in her drowsing. He bent his head, brushing her mouth with his, arousing her...

He wanted her again.

How long he would want her, now that he had her here with him, he did not know. Perhaps he would tire of her eventually. But he would not think about that. One thing he did know was that this time *she* would not be leaving *him*. He would make it impossible for her to want to do so. Not this time.

She had rejected him once but she would not do so again. While he desired her she would *crave* him—he would make very, very sure of that.

His hand smoothed over her flank, then her thigh, and eased inwards into the vee of her body...her quickening body... He heard her moan and gave a soft laugh, letting his fingers go where her slackening thighs told him she wanted them to go.

He heard her moan again and felt his own desire mount and harden. His body moved over hers, possessing her once more.

CHAPTER SEVEN

TALIA SIGHED LANGUOROUSLY and gave a rueful laugh. 'I feel so guilty! I really should be getting on with my designs!'

Luke reached for her hand. 'There's no rush,' he said lazily. 'I haven't even bought the site yet.'

Talia turned her head towards him. They were both relaxing on padded sun loungers, set beside the turquoise swimming pool beneath the shade of a wide parasol which protected them against the heat of the afternoon sun beating down on the lush gardens.

'You are going to buy it, though, aren't you?'

Was there urging in her tone? Whatever it was that had called to her in that sad, ruined place, she knew that she wanted it to be saved and restored, that it was important to bring it back to life again.

Luke squinted at her. 'Do you want me to?' he asked in the same lazy voice.

'Oh, yes!' she answered. 'It could be made *so* beautiful again!'

He nodded in assent. 'For a great deal of money, yes...' he agreed dryly. 'At the moment I'm still haggling over the price.' His tone sharpened slightly. 'The site owners are thinking I'm a rich foreign investor they can fleece for their own profit. *That*,' he said, and now there was a grim note in his voice, 'is their mistake.'

Talia glanced at him. It was unnerving to hear that change of tone, the hard, cold edge to it, and it sent a flicker of unease through her. She banished it, her expression softening. The Luke who had been so cold, so cruel and distant, had gone. He had vanished utterly and now—oh, now he was the man she remembered...the warm, passionate man who had swept her into his arms, showering her with kisses.

And, bliss beyond bliss, there was nothing to part them. She was here, with him, just as they'd dreamed of being—here in the sun-drenched Caribbean, in a tropical idyll to embrace them both. Before, it had been impossible—but now they could be together.

She felt emotion melt within her like warm honey and squeezed Luke's hand that was holding hers, just for the joy of knowing they lay hand in hand. He answered her gesture, lifting her hand to his mouth and kissing it softly, his eyes entwining with hers.

'I think we've had enough of the great outdoors for now, don't you?'

There was a husk in his voice, one that she was now thrillingly familiar with, and a speaking look in his dark, expressive eyes. He let his lips play over her hand, deliberately and sensuously exploring the tips of her fingers, softly biting at the mound of Venus below her thumb, brushing the delicate skin over her wrist.

She felt arousal beckon, her blood quicken, and her eyes clung to his. 'What did you have in mind?' she asked, her voice a soft tease.

He answered with a low laugh. 'Come inside and find out,' he challenged.

As he spoke, he swung his bare legs round and drew her upright. He slid a hand warm from the sun around her slender waist.

'If the staff weren't around you could find out right here,' he taunted. His hand slid from her waist over her rounded bottom, shaping it lazily. His eyes glinted. 'Tomorrow,' he said, 'we go shopping. This one-piece suit has got to go—I want you in a bikini. Or in nothing at all.'

His voice was a growl of arousal now and

Talia laughed, her eyes never leaving him. She ran a finger along the waistline of his trunks, letting it slip a little within, and laughed again at the sudden flexing of his muscles at her touch.

'That goes for me, too,' she answered. 'These trunks conceal far, *far* too much.'

Daringly, she started to ease her hand downwards—only for his lightning-fast grip to stay her.

'Don't!' he said, his voice dangerously taut.

It gave Talia a thrill of pleasure to know how very near to the edge of his control he was. Then, with a gasp, she was being hefted up into his arms.

He laughed in triumph and possession. 'Time to get you upstairs!' he exclaimed. 'Before I throw caution to the wind and ravish you here on the sun loungers!'

She snaked her arms around his neck, glorying in the strength of his body. 'Take me, I'm yours!' she cried with mock melodrama, laughing in return.

He strode indoors, carrying her as if she were a featherweight, sweeping her upstairs to take her and make her his—*all* his.

Luke leant forward against the deck railing on the yacht, gazing across to the shore.

Beside him, Talia gave a sigh of pleasurable appreciation. 'This is *so* gorgeous,' she breathed.

Luke laughed. 'It's a bit of a cliché, a sunset cruise, but definitely worth it!'

There was a soft footstep behind him and he turned. The steward was coming up to them, bearing a tray that held an ice bucket in which a bottle of champagne was nestling and two flutes. He set the tray down on a table near them, and the ice bucket in a stand, then took himself off. Luke reached for the champagne bottle and with a deft hand opened it, filled the flutes.

The rich light from the setting sun bathed them as the stately yacht creamed across the cobalt waters, and the distant shore was emerald-green and thick with vegetation. She gave another sigh of pleasure. Of radiant joy. How wonderful this was!

And all because of Luke.

She smiled now, taking the flute he was handing her, drinking him in. He was looking lean and relaxed, in an open-necked pale blue shirt, cuffs turned back, and tan chinos with deck shoes. He was elegant and absolutely edible.

She felt her stomach curl, knowing how much she wanted him, how much she needed him, how much she wished she could stay with him for ever.

A tiny flicker of uncertainty plucked at her. It had been nearly a week since they'd arrived on the island—nearly a week since Luke had claimed her for his own again. It had been the most blissful week in her entire life. But into her head came an echo of what he'd said to her back in his office in Lucerne, that day she'd had to seek him out and beg him for forbearance on evicting them straight away.

He wanted her to be here in the Caribbean for a fortnight. But what then? She didn't know. Could only hope. Hope against hope that being with her was as wonderful for him as being with him was to her. That with nothing to keep them apart now they could stay together...

She felt a longing surge within her—a longing never to be without him. Did he feel it, too? Did he want her in his life as she wanted him? She could only hope—hope with all her being.

'We need to celebrate.' Luke was raising his champagne flute.

Talia looked at him questioningly. He nodded across to the shoreline they were gliding past, and as they rounded a small cape a beach opened up before them, a crescent of silver sand littered with fallen palms, and at the far end were the wrecked remains of the building she had last seen from the land.

'Oh, it's the hotel site!' she exclaimed. 'There it is!'

'Indeed it is,' Luke said beside her. He raised his flute to hers. 'And now,' he said, and there was open satisfaction in his voice, 'it is *my* hotel site!'

She whipped her head round, her face lighting up. 'Oh, Luke, that's wonderful! You've actually bought it!'

'I drove a hard bargain,' he said, 'but, yes, it's mine now.' He glanced down at her. 'Are you glad?'

'Yes! I'm so, so pleased! It needed rescuing!'

He gave a laugh. 'You sound very sentimental about it.'

'And why not?' she countered. 'If you hadn't bought it what would have happened to it?'

'It would have been demolished, probably. Or left to rot totally.'

'Oh, that's awful. It deserves much better.'

He was silent a moment. Then, 'Yes, it does.'

There was something in his voice she hadn't heard before, and she looked at him curiously.

Then, abruptly, he clinked his glass against

hers. 'So, drink up. Celebrate my latest acquisition.' His long lashes dropped over his dark, expressive eyes. 'It's almost as good as the first one I made earlier this week.'

She looked at him, not understanding.

He dipped his head and kissed her in a leisurely fashion. '*You've* been a wonderful acquisition,' he said softly.

She looked at him uncertainly. 'Is that what I am?' she asked. There was something in her voice and she wasn't sure what it was, knew only that she didn't want it to be there. Her eyes searched his but he was simply smiling down at her, appreciation in his open gaze.

'Drink up,' he said again, in a low voice. 'There's plenty more in the bottle. They'll be serving our sunset supper at any moment.' His voice changed, grew husky. 'And after that I have every intention of testing out the bed in the stateroom down below.'

And he kissed her again, in that leisurely, casually possessive fashion…

It was good to kiss her. So very good to feel that velvet mouth of hers open to his, to taste its sweetness, savour its honey. To arouse the passion that came as he deepened his kiss.

But not right now. That was for later. For now he drew back, taking another draught of champagne, gazing out in a proprietorial fashion over the property he'd signed the purchase contract for that afternoon. For now he wanted to savour the moment. He wanted to savour everything.

He had bought the ruined hotel at the price *he* had wanted to pay—not the one that had been anticipated from him. It had been a fair price—but a keen one. Restoration would be expensive, as he had told Talia, and it would be years before he would see payback on the investment. But it would be worth it—and not just from a financial point of view.

His gaze went across the water to the lush shoreline. Why had it called to him so much, that derelict building battered into ruin by Nature's formidable, pitiless forces?

But he didn't really have to ask why. He knew.

As he gazed across the water another shoreline came into his mind—one that was as familiar to him as the back of his hand. One that he had seen countless times from his boyhood dinghy, tacking back and forth across the bay. Finally tiring, or driven by hunger—or both—he'd head downwind to beach his craft on the sandy shore, where he would haul it out of the water and then lope back to the low-rise century-old building that had been his home. His parents' home. His grandparents' before them, and another generation before them, as well.

Villa Xenakis, which had become the Hotel Xenakis, was lovingly transformed by his parents into a small but gracious beachside hotel, filled with carefully garnered antiquities and family heirlooms.

It had been a bijou hotel, just right for the discerning traveller wending his way through the myriad islands of the Aegean, filled with charm, character, and heritage. There had been arched doorways set into thick walls, paved terraces edged with huge ceramic *pithoi*, tumbling with vibrant flowers—scarlet and white geraniums, crimson and yellow bougainvillea, glossy-leaved miniature olive trees.

Little stone fountains had cooled the air... shady pergolas had been wound all about with honeysuckle and jasmine. There had been the endless chirruping of cicadas and by day it had been hot, but then had come the starlit nights, the soft lapping of the sea by the water's edge...

He blinked and the view was gone. Reduced to ruins.

His face shadowed. Nature had struck with all its callous fury, just like the hurricane that had destroyed the hotel he had purchased. But it had been no wind that had destroyed his

precious sanctuary. No, it had been an earthquake that had shaken his parents' hotel to its
foundations, collapsing half the roof and the
ceilings, shattering walls, turning the kitchens to rubble and the graceful archways to a
heap of broken stone.

But it had not been the earthquake that had
stolen his home from his parents and left them
with nothing. That had been done not by the
gods, or Nature, but by man. By one man.

He moved away from the rail, turning
abruptly. He would not think of that—not now.
He refused to think of the man who had stolen
from his parents all they'd held most dear. He
had got his revenge and that man was gone.
Destroyed by his avenging hand.

'Luke?'

Talia's voice at his side was hesitant, her
hand on his stiffened arm tentative. For a moment he looked down at her, at her upturned
face. But it was not her face he beheld.

It was her father's.

His eyes darkened, but with an effort he
cleared his expression.

*It's not her fault—not her fault she's his
daughter. I cannot blame her for being that.*

He would not let it trouble him. Not now.
Not when he had finally made her his.

He rested his eyes on her with appreciation in his gaze. It was not just her beauty that drew him, incandescent though it was—it was so much else, as well. He tried to analyse it, and failed, and then he didn't care that he couldn't analyse it. All he knew was that he could spend time with her and never be bored or restless, that whatever they talked about the conversation flowed between them, easy and spontaneous, just as it had that very first evening they'd met.

He was enjoying this relaxed, easy-going time with her—enjoying the fact that he could put his arm around her shoulder and she would lean in, or take her hand and she would squeeze his and smile at him, a warm and wonderful smile. He took delight in simply watching her move, in listening to her voice, in simply being with her.

Whatever it is she does to me it is something that no other woman can.

It was a truth he accepted now. And all he wanted to do was celebrate that truth.

He had come a long way to reach this point in his life. He had avenged his parents, destroyed his enemy, and he had even—his smile was wry—stepped in to save that devastated hotel, as if in tribute to the lost pride and joy of his parents, the legacy he had never inherited.

And now he was ready for this time with Talia.

He tilted his flute to hers, hearing the crystal ring out softly. His eyes met her upturned gaze, warming as they did.

'To us,' he said. 'To our time together.'

And life felt very, very sweet.

Talia was working. She was out on the balcony of her bedroom—not that she slept there any longer, for after that first night with Luke she always shared his bed. He was leaving her to work as she wanted, and she was glad.

Her eyes shadowed for a moment. Though he'd never referred to it again, it was clear that he judged her by the work she'd done for her father. But that fact only made her burn to show him that she was capable of better. And she was, she knew, for she was fizzing with unleashed creativity, inspired by the ruined majesty of the hotel, and she was rejoicing in it. She would make that sad, crumbling hotel come alive and show Luke just how beautiful it could be—in harmony with nature, as vivid and vibrant as its setting between the rainforest and the sea.

She worked on, busily and fruitfully, making the most of this time to herself, wanting to be as productive as she could be. Luke was away from the villa, interviewing architects, project managers, structural engineers—all the technical personnel who would be necessary to render the building sound again. Only when the empty shell was ready and waiting for her could her ideas start to take reality.

Once she had the artwork done, though, she wanted to head into the island's capital, to see what she would be able to source locally. She wanted to discover as much as she could about fabrics and designs that were in harmony with the island's heritage, its people, their culture. She'd already consulted Fernando and his wife, Julie, who was the housekeeper, and they had given her some good potential leads to follow up. In a small community like this one, there was so much untapped potential in local knowledge.

She felt her enthusiasm firing up a notch and it buzzed in her veins. She paused to look out across the vista, at the fabulous hillside view across the emerald-green landscape down to the azure sea. How beautiful it was! The whole world was beautiful—*her* world was beautiful. Her existence was blissful.

Because of Luke.

Luke had lit up her life and set her heart glowing with a fire that she could never quench—never wanted to quench. She sang his name in her head—more than just his name.

I'm in love with him.

As she gazed out over the vista before her she felt her breath catch as the realisation hit her. The truth of what she felt for him vibrated in her head as gloriously as his name! A rush of emotion fused through her. Of *course* she was in love with him! How could she not be? How could she not be in love with the man whose every touch thrilled her? Her expression softened with tenderness and recollection. The man with whom she felt so at ease.

That time of painful conflict between them had vanished. How had it ever existed, she wondered, when now the glow of warmth in his eyes never faded? How wonderful he was! How he made her smile, and laugh, made her feel carefree when he caught her to him and held her close, so close that she could feel the beat of his heart against hers!

Of course I'm in love with him! How could I not be?

She felt the rush of emotion come again, filling her being, and with it came another emotion, searing through her.

Hope.

Hope that if she was in love with him, then he might be in love with her.

Surely his passion for her, his ardour, cried out how much he felt—and not just in bed but all the time. The way he looked at her, took her hand, wound his arm around her, poured his gaze into hers, smiled at her, laughed with her... It was as if he could not get enough of her. And the way he nestled her against him, held her hand, meshed his fingers with hers, as if he would never let her go... Surely he felt the same?

She felt her breath catch again. A sigh of hope, of happiness, of sheer delight, escaped her as she breathed his name again.

In a dreamy-eyed reverie she reached for her colours again, more determined than ever to do her very best work for Luke.

A couple of hours later, a discreet cough behind her broke her concentration. It was Fernando, bringing a tray of tea for her, and she took a grateful break as the sun lowered to the horizon. Later she would ready herself for the evening. Luke was taking her out, and she wanted to dazzle him.

Julie had skilfully altered her evening gown for her, ridding it of all the frills and flounces. Its simple style had a sensual impact which she knew Luke would prefer.

Talia studied her appearance in the long mirror before heading downstairs for the evening, looking at her dramatic eye make-up and the long, loosened tresses of her hair tumbling over her shoulders.

She wished she could add some jewellery, but she had none. She'd never really had any, according to the lawyers who had brutally informed her that both her and her mother's jewellery were classed as a corporate asset, since her father had bought it with company funds and claimed it against tax.

Not, she thought with sudden bitterness, that it had been given to her by her father out of affection, but only because his daughter, like his wife, needed to be draped in expensive baubles to reflect his own success in life. They had been tokens of his wealth, not of his love.

She shook the memory from her, and forgot it completely in the glow of appreciation in Luke's eyes as she walked down the wide sweep of the staircase.

He closed in on her. 'Maybe we should postpone dinner,' he murmured, and the familiar husk in his voice sent a little thrill of arousal through Talia. Then he released her. 'No, I want to enjoy looking at you all evening and delay my gratification. The reward will come later.' His dark eyes glinted with open desire. 'And will be all the sweeter for it.'

He handed her into the waiting limo.

'Where are we going?' Talia asked.

He laughed. 'We're going to try the place you flounced out of and see if we can have a better time there tonight.'

Talia smiled. It was a certainty that they would enjoy the evening a million times more than the disastrous first time.

And so it proved.

This time Talia was as relaxed as she had been tense before. Now, as they took their places at their table, she gazed about the room with equanimity.

Luke followed her gaze. He frowned inwardly, remembering that first evening. when he had discovered how completely unqualified and inexperienced Talia was to undertake what he'd so rashly invited her here to do.

His expression softened. Well, he would come up with some tactful way of hiring a designer who *was* up to the task, and in the meantime, if it brought Talia pleasure to dabble with her colours and paints, imagining she was doing something useful with the time she was spending on dreaming up her designs, then he was happy to indulge her.

Just as her father had, he realised with another inward frown.

With a rich, doting father, Talia would have been allowed to imagine herself useful to her darling daddy, however hopeless she actually was. As witnessed by the dire interiors of all the Grantham properties. Tasteless, ostentatious, and 'cookie-cutter'—showing not a trace of flair or originality or style.

Impatiently, he cleared his unwelcome thoughts. His interest in Talia was not in her professional talents—or lack of them.

His expression softened and he reached for her hand across the table. 'Have I told you yet how incredibly delectable you look tonight?' he asked, a smile in his voice and his eyes. His gaze glanced over her. 'That dress is spectacular!' he breathed, his eyes lingering on the generous cleavage that it exposed.

Talia laughed. 'It's the same dress I wore that first time here. Julie altered it for me. I think it's a huge improvement, and if you do too then we're both pleased.'

Luke frowned. 'You shouldn't have had to do that. We'll go shopping tomorrow,' he announced decisively.

'Can we?' she asked eagerly. 'I really want to start checking out what I can source for the refurb here on the island. Fernando's been kind enough to make some suggestions as to shops I can look at, for fabrics and so on.'

'If that's what you want,' Luke agreed equably. It would do no harm, after all, and if it kept her happy then he would give her her head. 'But we'll try the boutiques first. There's an upmarket mall not far from here—you'll be able to find some of your usual designers there, I'm sure.'

She was looking at him uncertainly. 'I... I don't really think I should. I've got a wardrobe full of designer dresses at the Marbella villa. I didn't bring any of them with me because I thought I'd be here to work, and I wouldn't really need any evening wear.'

'Well, you do,' Luke replied decisively. 'Although...' his voice dropped, taking on a sensual twist '... I far prefer you with nothing on at all.'

The arrival of the service staff put paid to any further explication and he settled back to order. This time they would enjoy the Michelin-starred delights on the extensive menu—and the prestigious wine cellars. This time nothing would mar their evening.

Nor did it.

In the luxurious surroundings of the five-star hotel, both he and Talia enjoyed a leisurely meal and then, repairing to the terrace which overlooked the hotel's private beach, they settled down with liqueurs and coffee. What they talked about Luke couldn't remember— he knew only that conversation flowed easily, as it always did now.

Eventually they made a move. Luke's arm came around her shoulder and she nestled into his casual embrace. As they made their way back to the lobby, along a wide, marble-tiled concourse, Luke paused beside one of the several exclusive boutiques that lined each side.

'Want to look in?' He smiled. 'We could make a start on your new wardrobe.'

The store was still open, even at this late hour, for the hotel's patrons might wish to make purchases at any time. The window display sported several svelte evening gowns, all of which would have looked spectacular on Talia. But she shook her head.

'Way too late,' she said, and smiled.

Then her eye was caught by something. On a separate plinth in the window was a display of jewellery. She lingered another moment. One of the pieces—a showy diamond and pearl pendant—looked like the one her father had bestowed upon her for a birthday a few years ago. Her expression flickered.

'Does that take your fancy?' Luke asked in a genial tone.

'It's like one my father gave me,' she heard herself say. Then she cut herself short. She didn't want to think about it.

Her father had only ever presented jewellery to her when her mother was present, and Talia had had to exclaim in surprise and delight at his generosity. It would always elicit some comment from her mother about how wonderful her father was, how generous he was to them.

Talia shuddered at the hypocrisy of her response, at how her father had made her collude with his flattering image of himself lest her mother be upset. Her mother had always needed to go on believing in the fiction that they were a happy family, that hers was a happy marriage. She'd never been able to face the brutal truth of it.

'I think that would suit you better.'

Grateful for Luke's interruption of her troubled thoughts, Talia looked to where he was indicating a ruby bracelet, glittering under the spotlight highlighting the display.

'Oh, that is *beautiful*!' Talia exclaimed spontaneously, for the delicate array of rich red gems forming a continuous loop was indeed breathtakingly lovely in its stylish simplicity.

Then something else caught her eye. A watch—a man's watch, judging by its size and design—its face and casing almost completely obliterated with diamonds.

She giggled—she couldn't stop herself. 'Oh, Luke, do look!' She cast him a mischievous glance. 'Now, you *have* to admit that's a lot less dull than *your* boring watch!'

She touched with her finger the sombre, understated, formidably elegant—and ferociously expensive—custom-made watch that he always wore. Memory played at her—how she'd noticed it at that party, made some comment about it, and he had said it had been a reward for himself.

With an inner shiver she realised with hindsight just what the reason for that costly indulgence had been.

He had been celebrating taking over Grantham Land.

That inner shiver came again. Her father, too, had liked to celebrate any major kill he'd made in the marketplace. A new car—the latest model of whatever was the most expensive brand at the time—had been his favoured object of conspicuous display, his way of showing off his success to the world.

Again, she was grateful as Luke replied to her deliberately teasing comment.

'Diamonds would look better on you than me,' he said dryly. He squeezed her shoulder. 'Come on—stop drooling like a magpie!' His voice changed, grew husky. 'I want to get you home.'

He paused to drop a kiss on her mouth—

lingering enough to let her know why he was so keen to get her home, just swift enough to keep it decent in public.

But as he bore her off across the lobby to get her into the car, so he wouldn't have to care about public behaviour, he found himself glancing back at the display of glittering jewellery. So she liked the ruby bracelet?

A smile flickered around his mouth as he walked by her side.

Well, why not? He was in the mood to be indulgent.

CHAPTER EIGHT

'I'LL TAKE A swatch of this one, and this… and this. And that one. And let's try that one as well.' Talia smiled as the woman nodded, reaching for her scissors to cut the strips of fabric that her customer had selected.

Talia got out her notebook, noting the fabric names and colours, then checking the price per metre for each of them and adding that too. She tapped the book in satisfaction. There—that was a start. And it was looking promising.

She launched into a technical discussion with the woman, of widths and weights and thread counts and finishes. This was where she was in her element, and she was loving it. Loving being able to get totally stuck in to the next stage of turning her creative vision into reality.

The saleswoman was enthusiastic—as well she might be, Talia acknowledged, given the value of her custom if Luke were to agree to her proposals.

Oh, please let him like what I've come up with. Please let him agree with my vision for the place! I so, so want it to be beautiful and for him to love it like I do.

She knew she had to be careful in her costings. Luke had made it very clear he wanted value for money. Her mouth tightened in grim memory. But she was used to having to justify every pound she spent. Her father had always given her the tightest budget he could get away with, and there had never been any question that he would tolerate her exceeding it by so much as a penny.

She shook her head free of unpleasant memories. Her work here was completely different. This was a labour of love.

She smiled to herself. Thoughts fluttered deep inside, in a place she scarcely dared acknowledge. A labour of love, indeed—and not just for the sake of bringing back to vivid, vibrant life that sad, hurricane-blasted hotel.

It was for Luke's sake.

The man she loved.

Her smile became rueful. Out of love, she had let him do what she knew she shouldn't have that very morning.

As promised, he'd taken her to the upmarket shopping mall he'd mentioned, getting her to choose two more evening gowns, several sundresses, and a handful of ultra-brief bikinis and diaphanous wraps. She'd tried not to see the price tickets, for she knew she should not have let him buy such expensive things for her, but he had been insistent, and it had so obviously given him pleasure to do it.

So she'd squared her conscience by telling herself that she'd be wearing them for *him*, not for herself—that it would be to bring into his eyes that light of open appreciation that she so loved to see...the one that turned so swiftly to sensual desire.

She quivered with the little thrill that kicked in her pulse simply at the memory of how he could make her feel and how he made her respond. She gloried in it. It was like walking on air, floating in a haze of happiness. This was really happening to her; the man of her dreams was making her his own.

She all but skipped out of the shop, checking the time. Luke had left her to her own devices after they'd lunched at a beachfront restaurant, heading off for yet another meeting with architects and planning officials. But they were to meet for sundowner cocktails at a fashionable bar by the marina, and she quickened her step, for she still had more calls to make.

She was seeking out furniture, window treatments, bedding, and crockery—and then, if local suppliers didn't prove possible, a couple of import-expert companies to handle bringing goods in from abroad, all of which would require precise costings and copious paperwork. But she would include it all in what she presented to Luke—and hope that it would convince him to use her designs.

Multiple calls kept her busy, and by the time she reached the cocktail bar at the end of the afternoon Luke was already in the open-air lounge, looking sinfully relaxed, his long legs stretched out in front of him, a ferocious-looking margarita in his hand. He wore even more ferociously expensive sunglasses that made her go weak at the knees.

'Had fun?' he enquired lazily.

'Hugely!' She laughed, sitting herself down and ordering a fruit-based rum cocktail from the immediately attentive waiter. She fished inside one of her carrier bags. 'Do you want to see some of the materials I'm sampling?' she asked.

Luke waved his glass in negation. 'Not right now,' he said casually.

He didn't want to sound dismissive. She'd clearly had an enjoyable session—choosing colours and fabrics, or whatever it was she thought passed for work—but he didn't want his time wasted over something hopelessly amateurish, and he couldn't bear to have his infatuation with her diminished if she brought out tasteless designs. He wouldn't be able to lie and smile and pretend it was good work. If what she was going to produce was anything like what she'd done for her father's buildings then she had absolutely no eye for colour, style, or shape.

He'd eventually have to get around to hiring a professional designer and handing the work over to them to produce something suitable. However, he had no wish to hurt Talia's feelings, so he softened his rejection by laughing gently.

'And in return I promise not to tell *you* about how irritating I find planning officials!' He took another mouthful of his margarita. 'But from now on I'm leaving all that to the project manager I've appointed. He can cope with officialdom. Besides—'

He broke off. He'd been about to say that he wouldn't be spending much more time here on the island. Buying the hotel site had been an impulse, catching at something deep within him. But his business life was conducted in the financial centres of the world. That was where he'd made the fortune he'd had to make in order to forge the weapon he'd needed to bring down his enemy.

His fingers clenched over the stem of his cocktail glass and forcibly he made them relax again. Grantham was destroyed. And everything the man had once possessed was now his.

His eyes skimmed over the woman at his side, sipping delicately from the multi-coloured cocktail she'd been served.

Everything he had is mine now. Even his daughter.

His eyes were shadowed behind his sunglasses. He would have given a great deal for Talia *not* to be Gerald Grantham's daughter. His mouth tightened. But he would not blame her for what she could not help.

His eyes skimmed over her now. She was wearing one of the floaty, floral sundresses he'd bought for her that morning. It had been formidably expensive, though she hadn't even glanced at the price tag. Of course for Gerald Grantham's daughter price tags had never been of any concern.

But he would not blame her for that, either. It was what she was used to—of course she took it for granted. Why shouldn't she? It was the habit of a lifetime.

But not one she can afford any longer.

Unless, of course, there was another man to provide it for her.

The thought hung in his mind, but he knew what must come next.

It is what she will want—what she will expect. And if I want her I have to accept that.

He raised his cocktail to his lips, taking another mouthful. What they had was worth it—oh, more than worth it. He must accept her as she was—as he had done when he hadn't known she was Gerald Grantham's daughter.

His eyes rested on her again and instinctively he took her hand, feeling her fingers press his in return, watching her mouth parting in a fond smile at his gesture. His gaze softened in automatic response. Tonight—this very night—he would make his feelings for her clear.

And what her answer would be he already knew.

She will never leave me again. Never.

The certainty warmed in his eyes and he meshed his fingers with hers, entwining them together, sure in his possession of this most irresistible of women. So very, very special.

And tonight I will show her just how special she is. I will show her exactly what she means to me...

It was a good feeling.

* * *

Slowly, with deliberate control, Luke let his fingertips trail down the valley between the ripe orbs of Talia's lush breasts. His fingers splayed out across the slender softness of her body and then, with even more deliberate control, he slipped them between her thighs.

She gave a low moan of pleasure and he lowered his mouth to the crested peaks of her breasts, adoring each in turn as more moans came from her arching throat. His own arousal was complete, and he was ready—more than ready—for his possession of her. With the same absolute self-control he moved his body over hers.

Afterwards, as their heart rates slowed and their breathing eased in the exhausted torpor that had come to them, Luke settled her into the crook of his arm, feeling her body warm and drowsy against his, their limbs still tangled. Above them, the slow blades of the ceiling fan rotated lazily, cooling the ambient air, though not enough for him to need to reach for the coverlet which had slumped to the floor.

Lightly, his hand brushed the soft contours of her rounded hip, then trailed over her slender thigh. 'Do you realise,' he murmured, 'that we've been here on the island nearly two weeks?'

Did he feel her tense suddenly? If he did, he was glad of it. It gave him reason to continue. His life had changed utterly since Talia had walked into his office, and he wanted to keep it that way. He could not—*would* not—lose her again.

He dropped a soft kiss on her forehead, smiling. 'Tempting though it is, I can't stay here lotus-eating for ever,' he went on. 'I've got to the point now where I can leave the restoration of the hotel to the experts I've appointed, and it's time to pick up my life.'

He took a breath, his hand on her hip tightening slightly.

'So what do you say to coming with me to Hong Kong? Then on to Shanghai? I've got various matters I have to see to there—business matters—but after that...' his voice warmed '...maybe we could drop down to the South Seas and explore the islands there?'

He took another breath, and then he said what had been burning in him for days.

'I want you with me, Talia—wherever in the world I go. Will you come with me? Stay with me?'

He paused, levering himself up on his elbow, looking down at her. Waiting for her answer.

For a moment there was absolute silence. Then, with a cry, she flung her arms around him.

'Yes! Oh, yes. Oh, Luke, yes! Yes, yes, *yes*!'

Her voice was full of a joy that blazed like the sun, and Luke's heart felt suddenly whole for the first time he could remember.

Talia was floating on air. She was ten feet up, soaring with happiness. There were things she would have to sort out first—she knew that. Before she could take off for her very own personal paradise with Luke. But with Luke now committed to her she felt no apprehension about explaining to him about her poor mother, how she must ensure she was safely settled and secure in her future. Surely Luke would see that? Surely he would let her mother stay on in the Marbella villa for as long as she wanted, once she told him about her health condition?

She would take Luke to meet her when they were back from the Far East. Luke would reassure her, and she knew her mother would be overjoyed that her daughter had found love and happiness.

It's the happily-ever-after that I've always longed for!

All day she continued floating on air, even

though she saw little of Luke. He'd incarcerated himself in his office, telling her he had work to get on with, but he had said they would celebrate that evening, and asked her to confer with Julie and Fernando to lay on a suitable celebratory feast for dinner.

Talia didn't mind that Luke was working, because she was, too. Gathering all the samples she'd collected the day before in the island's capital, she settled down on her bedroom balcony to produce her colour board, happily humming away to herself as she did so, referring back to her sketches and annotating everything with the costing notes she'd made and the calculations she'd run.

She was kept busy all day on the internet, researching for furniture, window treatments, and bed linens, and all the other myriad requirements that would be needed, whittling them down to a shortlist before she printed out photos and added copious notes and yet more costings.

As the sun was setting they shared a late swim in the pool—Luke vigorously ploughing up and down, Talia contenting herself with some gentle breaststroke. Then she left Luke to it while she headed back upstairs to get ready for the evening ahead.

She all but floated up the stairs. And back down again, some two hours later.

She had dressed with exceptional care, her heart beating fit to burst, and knew that she looked as beautiful as it was possible for her to look.

Julie, emerging from the kitchens, clapped her hands, and Fernando smiled benignly and ushered her through to the terrace, where Luke was waiting for her.

For a moment he did not speak, and then he came up to her, reaching for her hands. 'How can you be so beautiful?' he breathed, his eyes warm upon her, lighting up her face, her eyes, her smile, like the moon and the stars.

She was wearing another of the new gowns he'd bought for her the day before, this one more formal than the one she'd worn the previous evening. It was in pale blue silk, with a very fine plissé texture, and it cupped her breasts almost like a strapless bikini top, then fell in graceful folds to her ankles.

He himself was in a tux, but he had slung his jacket and tie over a chair in the close warmth of the evening. He looked elegant, roguish, and—Talia gave a little gulp of sheer attraction—unbearably gorgeous...

He handed her to her seat at the table, which had been beautifully set by Julie, with scented flowers rioting all over, candles sheltered by glass containers, crystal and silver sparkling in their light. Beside the table champagne nestled in ice on a stand, already opened and smoking gently.

Luke hefted the bottle out, filled their glasses.

'To us,' he said. His gaze was lambent, rich with expression.

Much later, Talia rested her cheek against Luke's bare chest. Her heart rate was easing, her breathing slowing. Yet her whole body was still glowing, flushed with the aftermath of her physical ecstasy.

How can it be so incredible? Every time!

Wonder still filled her at what Luke could arouse in her—an explosion not just of the most intense pleasure possible, but of an intense joy that flowered in her heart.

She felt her soul soar, turning over and over in ecstasy.

I love him so much. How can I love him so much?

She did not know—only knew that she did. And that giving herself to him with all that she possessed, with all that she was, had transformed her life utterly and completely.

Did he love her?

The question was there—she had faced it, accepted she could have no answer yet. Perhaps he did, but did not yet realise it? Or perhaps he was still growing towards it? Letting it steal upon him as it had for her?

But he would come to love her—of that she was certain. Men took longer to realise their emotions—she knew that…everyone knew that. It was common knowledge. They told of their emotions in deeds, not words. And with everything Luke did, and the way he was with her, he demonstrated just how precious she was to him. After all, he'd asked her to travel with him, to *stay* with him…

She gave a sigh of happiness, wrapping her arm around his strong, lean waist. How gorgeous he was…how unutterably gorgeous. And how impossible it was, she thought, to be anything except blissfully, wonderfully happy! She and Luke were together. Building a life together—*always* together!

Nothing can part us now. Nothing.

The certainty of it filled her as she nestled into him, glowing with radiant happiness and love, revelling in the warmth of his arm around her back, folding her to him, and knowing with every fibre of her being how absolutely perfect her happiness was. And how she gloried in it!

She gave another sigh of bliss and pure, perfect happiness, then felt his arm move and reach out past her; heard the noise of his bedside table drawer sliding open. Her eyes fluttered open as she felt Luke shift position, drawing back so that he was half propped against the pillows. She raised her head to meet his gaze, which was drawing down towards her in the soft light from the lamp.

'I have something for you,' he said, and his smile was warm, his eyes warmer still.

He lifted the box he'd taken from the drawer, flicking it open with his hand.

Talia gasped. She couldn't help it. Catching the lamplight, the ruby bracelet glittered with a crimson fire that seemed to burst from the heart of each precious gem.

'For you,' said Luke. A half-smile tugged at his mouth. 'I would have given it to you at dinner, but it would not have matched that blue gown. But now…' his mouth dipped to graze her shoulder '…it will suit you perfectly. Just as you are.'

He lifted her hand, took the bracelet from its velvet case and draped it around her slender wrist, fastening it.

'It fits you perfectly,' he said. He smiled again. 'I had it delivered this afternoon. It's the one from the hotel that you so admired. It's yours. Yours to keep.'

He kissed her mouth, sealing his gift to her. Then he eased her body back against his. Her hand lay on his chest, glittering with the bracelet's fiery gems. They seemed to glow against her skin.

The bracelet had been expensive—overpriced, he knew—but then it was priced for a hotel concession, and the impulse buys that men like him would be likely to make when on holiday with a woman they desired and cherished. He hadn't cared about the mark-up—only wanted to bestow upon the woman he was going to take with him now wherever he went something she had shown she desired. To show her that he wanted to give her what she desired.

He heard her speak, and expected to hear an expression of delight. But it was not.

'Why…why have you given this to me?'

There was a note of incomprehension in her voice. Of doubt. He kissed her again. He wanted only to experience the joy of giving her something that showed her how precious she was to him.

'To make you beautiful for me!' he said lightly.

Then, knowing it was time to say more, he

looked down at her, cupping her face with his hand. His voice would be serious now. He had to say what needed to be said—what had to be acknowledged if they were to continue together now.

'Talia, I know how difficult it has been for you since your world crashed about you. Losing your father...' His voice held an edge. 'I think we both know he isn't coming back. And even if he did—' that edge was harder now '—he would be penniless. No use to you at all. But whether or not he ever does show up again, nothing can take away how hugely traumatic this time has been for you. I understand that.'

He took a breath, knowing it was time to confront the unspoken truths that lay heavy between them. If they were to make a life together they had to be addressed and dealt with so they could move on together.

'You went from wealth to poverty overnight—the kind of poverty you were never equipped to deal with. You are the daughter of a very wealthy man, who doted on you and spoiled you, and I understand that the life you have been reduced to now is unimaginable for you. All your life you've been sheltered, as only the daughter of a rich man can be. And I know and I understand—truly I do, Talia—

that your situation is something you find incredibly hard to accept. I want you to know that I don't blame you for that. You are not responsible for your upbringing, nor for taking for granted the way of life your father's wealth allowed you to have. It would be harsh of me—unfair of me—to judge you for that. You can't help being the way you are, for being *what* you are—a rich man's daughter who has had everything provided for her all her life. A life of luxury and ease. It's no wonder you don't understand how brutal and tough the world can be.'

His expression changed.

'That day you came to me at my offices in Lucerne, expecting me to give you what you wanted, I was tough on you. I didn't make allowances for you and I should have. But now I *do* make those allowances. And, just as it wasn't fair of me to expect you to be able to do secretarial work for me, so it wasn't fair of me to expect you to try and take on something as major as a complete hotel refit.'

He picked his words carefully, for he did not want to hurt her feelings.

'I realise that your father let you enjoy trying out your design ideas on his properties, and that he indulged you in this, but I would hate for you to spend any more time with your paints and fabrics, however much you've been enthusing over them.' He smiled at her with fond affection. 'The hotel is a major project—a huge amount of work will be involved—and I'll be hiring a firm of professionals at some point to take it on.'

He smiled again, trying to be tactful.

'You don't have to worry about it any more. Besides, you won't have time to do anything like that—not if you're going to be with me from now on. I'd far rather you spent all your time and energy on *me*!' he said lightly, keeping his tone humorous, so as not to upset her.

Then, in a more serious vein, having—he hoped—explained to her as gently as he could why she no longer had to feel she should work for him, he went on. This was the key message he needed her to absorb—the message that would reassure her, that would ensure she was never tempted to leave him again. This was where he would explain that he would provide all she could ever want or need or dream of.

He softened his voice and stroked her hair, gazing down into her wide, wide eyes. 'Because, Talia, from now on you won't have to face the world on your own.' He dropped a tender kiss on her lips. 'From now on you'll have me to look after you. To take care of you.' His fingers dropped to the glittering ruby bracelet around her wrist where it lay across his chest, tapping it gently. 'This is a token— proof of how much I want you, of how much I want to take care of you. You can trust me, Talia, because of *this*. That's what I want you to know.'

He lifted his hand away and traced the soft outline of her parted lips as she lay gazing up at him. He could not read her expression, but that did not trouble him. She would be taking in his words, finding in them the reassurance he wanted her to have. The knowledge that she was safe to commit herself to him as she had not dared to do before,

'You won't have to leave me again, Talia. I know you did that first night, because you were afraid. Afraid to risk coming with me because you might have been disappointed. I was a stranger—you knew nothing about me other than that we lit fires inside each other. So you went back to the safety and the security of your existing life.'

His expression changed.

'I was angry with you then. For walking out on me. For rejecting me. But since then—since our time together—I've come to terms with it. And now that your old life is gone, now that it's behind you, I acknowledge…' He paused, and when he spoke again there was a rueful quality to his voice. It was guarded, as well. 'I freely admit that my actions caused the destruction of your former life. Maybe you can accept this bracelet as…as recompense?' His voice warmed and he gazed lovingly upon her. 'As my promise to you that I will take care of you from now on.'

He trailed his finger along the glittering gems once again.

'Rubies are beautiful, but so many other gemstones would suit you, too!' He relaxed back against the pillows, his hand cupping her shoulder affectionately. 'Hong Kong is brilliant for jewellery,' he told her. 'And how about a Tahitian pearl necklace when we explore the South Seas? Would you like that? Hand-picked from oysters of our own choosing!'

Talia was looking at him. There was something strange about her expression, and in her voice when she spoke. 'Oysters die when you take the pearls to make a necklace from them.'

He gave a rueful laugh. It was an odd thing for her to say, to be sure, but he had a reply for it all the same. 'There's a price to be paid for everything in life, Talia. No one can escape it.'

'Yes, you're right,' she said quietly. She lifted the hand which was weighed down by the ribbon of rubies and shifted her gaze to look at it.

'Do you like it?' Luke asked softly. He knew she did, but he wanted to hear her say so.

'It's beautiful. Exquisite,' she acknowledged, though her tone was unexpectedly flat.

His hand tightened around her shoulder. 'And so are you, Talia. Beautiful. Exquisite.'

There was a husk in his voice, a quickening in his limbs. He felt arousal stir and begin to take him over. He started to kiss her, opening her soft mouth to his, letting his free hand drop to her breast, moulding it with his palm until it peaked between his scissoring fingers.

She gave a low moan in her throat—a sound that was so familiar to him now that it served to heighten his own arousal. He moved his body over hers, beginning his possession. He would lose himself to this woman, and for some reason that no longer frightened him. He *wanted* to lose himself to her, this beautiful woman. She might be the daughter of his enemy, but that was behind them now that he had cleared the air.

A tide of passion flooded through him as he felt the facets of the rubies brush against his shoulder when she lifted her hand to snake it around the nape of his neck. He could feel her surrender to the passion flooding through her as powerfully as it was through him. Her fingers meshed into his hair, shaping his skull, deepening her own kisses.

His last conscious thought was, *She will never leave me now. Never.*

Triumph filled him. Triumph and absolute certainty.

Yet when he woke at dawn she was gone.

CHAPTER NINE

TALIA CLIMBED OUT of the taxi which had brought her from the train station. Her journey back to Marbella had been long and arduous. It had begun with her creeping from the villa, catching the early-morning bus to the capital, then taking another bus to the airport.

She had been reluctant to waste her meagre resources on taxis, and for the same reason she'd bought the cheapest flight available, which had meant multiple changes at various airports before she'd finally landed in Malaga to take the coastal train to Marbella.

Tiredness ate at her—and, worse than tiredness, a desolation of the spirit such as she had never known. She had thought she'd felt desolation before, on that morning after the party when she'd forced herself to leave the man who had swept her off her feet.

But that had not been desolation like this.

She felt again that crushing, stifling feeling

in her chest as she stepped inside the luxurious villa that was like a mocking ghost from a life that had ceased to exist.

Maria greeted her warmly, and with a grim effort Talia pasted a doggedly bright smile on her face. It was a smile that softened as she went out onto the terrace to find her mother relaxing in the shade, looking a hundred times healthier than when Talia had last set eyes on her.

'Mum—oh, you're looking *so* much better!' Relief flooded through Talia as she greeted her mother. It was the only good emotion she'd felt since—

She sheared her thoughts away. They had been agony for her all the way back here, and she could bear to think them no longer. Not now when she had to face her mother. When she had to hide the truth from her. When she had to hide what she had so nearly been reduced to. It had taken all her strength to reject Luke's promises and she could not bear to think about it.

'Well, I've Maria to thank for that.' Her mother smiled, encompassing the Spanish woman still beaming at Talia's return.

'I made sure she ate!' Maria pronounced.

'Oh, dear, I'm sure I've put on pounds!' Maxine Grantham admitted, as if that was a crime. But then, if her father had been here, for her mother to have gained even half a pound would indeed have been a crime.

'Do you think I want a fat wife?' he had berated her often enough, if he'd thought Maxine was looking anything less than fashionably stick-thin.

Talia's eyes darkened. As usual, her mother had done whatever it took to please the husband she was devoted to—including taking the slimming pills that had weakened her heart.

And what might I have done to please a man? The man I was devoted to until the veils were ripped from my eyes.

She sheared her mind away and silenced the pain inside.

'Well, it suits you—you look much healthier,' she said firmly to her mother, smiling brightly.

She would not let her mother think about her controlling husband. Instead she told her again how well she looked, and thanked Maria for her care of her.

Maria bustled off to make supper, refusing Talia's offer to help, leaving her to sit down beside her mother and enjoy the last of the evening sunshine. Low sunlight glinted on the pool beyond the terrace and bathed the garden in warmth.

'I'm so *glad* you're home, darling!' her mother exclaimed. 'Maria has been an angel, but I've missed you!' Her eyes lit up. 'Now, tell me—how did it go? Tell me all about it!'

Talia braced herself. She'd known her mother would ask questions—known she had to find something to say. Because it was the safest thing, she launched into a description of the island, knowing it would divert her mother. But as she rattled on pain and bitterness twisted inside her.

All the long journey home she'd kept hearing Luke's words to her. Words that had stripped from her the pathetic illusions she'd been building up. Words that had shown her— brutally and unambiguously—what he truly thought about her. Behind the smiles and the kisses and the passion there had always been this.

He had reduced her to the most abject and contemptible of human beings. He thought her a pampered doll, useless and worthless, totally talentless, amusing herself with pretending to be a designer. He thought she had a sky-high sense of entitlement and he believed she thought the world owed her not just a living but a deluxe lifestyle. The man she loved saw her as a spoiled princess, to be indulged and sheltered from life's vicissitudes, unable to cope with anything at all. A pet who had to be tossed bracelets and baubles to keep her happy, to make her feel valued and protected.

No! She couldn't bear to think of it! Couldn't bear to face what Luke truly thought of her.

She bit her lip to stop the emotional pain, making it physical instead.

'Darling, what is it?' Her mother's hand pressed on her arm. 'You look upset. Oh, darling girl, don't worry if you don't get the commission after all. It would be lovely if you did, but as soon as your father gets home we won't have to worry about anything like that any more. He'll be taking care of us again soon.'

Talia tensed, as if jerked on a wire.

'Mum, don't!' Her words were blurted out, harsh and angry.

Her mother looked hurt and shocked, and Talia tried to soften the impact. To hear her mother still mouthing such impossibilities, still believing in them, was galling. But it was more than that for Talia—her mother's words were an echo of Luke's promise.

Luke said he'd take care of me.

She hauled her mind away. She must not let herself hear those words in her head again. She had to banish him completely.

Pain and bitterness twisted again, and she

cast about to find some way of replying to her mother's useless longing.

'Mum, he's not coming back. You mustn't think that's going to happen. You have to face the truth.'

Her mother's expression hadn't changed. 'No, darling. We mustn't give up on him. We mustn't give up hope. He's simply sorting things out. He's off somewhere, making everything right again. You'll see. He'll be home soon and everything will be back to normal— just the way it should be. We'll get back our lovely home by the river and—'

Something snapped inside Talia. She couldn't stop herself. The gruelling journey had left her dog-tired physically—but infinitely worse was the despairing bleakness inside her, which had left her at the very edge of self-control. And now it snapped like an elastic band that had been stretched tighter and tighter.

She leapt to her feet. 'Mum, stop it! Just *stop it*! Dad isn't coming back. He's left us here to cope with nothing. No money, no assets—nothing. Everything's gone—including this villa.'

'No, don't say that—please. I can't bear it.'

Her mother's face had contorted and Talia cursed herself for losing her rag the way she had. Her mother couldn't cope with the brutal reality into which her husband's ruin and disappearance had forced them.

'You told me you'd sorted it all out,' her mother rushed on now. 'That the villa is ours.'

Talia closed her eyes in weariness and dejection. 'Only for three months, Mum. Just to give us time to find somewhere else to live… for you to get strong enough to face the truth of what Dad's done.'

A moan came from her mother, and Talia's dismay at her rash outburst deepened. But it was too late to stop now.

'We have to be grateful we can stay on even for that long. It was the deal I agreed—I would do some initial design work in the Caribbean in exchange for three months here in the villa to get you well and strong. I struck a bargain with Luke Xenakis—the man who now owns everything that's left of Grantham Land.'

Her mother's expression changed and her hand flashed out to grasp Talia's arm. 'You've been working for *that man*? That dreadful man who stole your father's company from him!' she gasped, aghast.

Talia sighed heavily. 'He didn't steal it, Mum—he just took it over. That's the way these business deals happen—'

'He *ruined* your father!' Maxine shot back.

'No, Mum. Dad did that himself. He went under because he took out more and more unsupported loans. Luke Xenakis just bought up what was left—which is why he's ended up owning everything that once belonged to Dad's company.'

Her mother's face contorted again. 'I don't care what you say happened—he ruined your father! How could you agree to work for him? How *could* you?'

'I told you, Mum. It was the only way to get him to let us stay on here until you're strong enough to move.'

'I can't bear it!' Maxine wailed, wringing her hands. 'To be beholden to that dreadful man! I hope you gave him a piece of your mind for what he's done to us?'

Talia rubbed her forehead. No, she had not given Luke a piece of her mind. She had given him everything else, but not that.

I gave him everything willingly, gloriously—my body, my soul. I would have gone anywhere with him, done anything for him.

But, she thought bitterly, she had concocted a fantasy in which he loved her the way she loved him. In which he knew her, respected her, believed in her…

I gave him my stupid, worthless heart, and all he wanted was me between the sheets.

A sob broke from her. She couldn't stop it. Couldn't stop the one that came after, either, which tore like barbed wire through her throat, choked from her, desperate and despairing.

'Darling!' Her mother's voice was different now. 'Darling, what is it? Oh, my darling, what's the matter? Was it that dreadful man? What did he do to you! Tell me, darling—tell me what he did to you.'

And, to Talia's mortification and tearful dismay, she broke into uncontrollable sobs and told her mother just how Luke Xenakis had broken her heart.

Luke was on his balcony. In his bedroom, his suitcase was being packed. Rage scythed in him. More than rage. Worse than rage. Blackness filled him, obliterating everything around.

She had done it to him again. She had walked out on him. Just upped and gone without a word. Not even a note this time.

But he hadn't needed a note to know the brutal truth. She did not want him. *Still* did not want him. She had rejected him—left him *again*.

His fists spasmed in the depths of his trouser pockets, his face contorting.

I did everything I could think of to make her happy. Everything!

This time he'd known who she was, *what* she was. That first time, after the party, he'd taken her at face value—had never dreamt in a million years that she would be Grantham's daughter, that she would be a pampered princess, the spoiled and indulged daughter of his sworn enemy. This time he'd known just what he needed to do to give her what she wanted, what she expected so that she would stay.

But she'd still walked out on him. Still rejected him.

He felt pain like a whiplash across his shoulders. Pain that was a thousand times worse than it had ever been that first time.

How could she walk out on me? After all those nights when we burned in each other's arms! After all those carefree days, the companionship, the togetherness?

But it had meant nothing to her—nothing at all!

Bitterness flowed in his veins like acid, etching into his flesh, consuming him from the inside out until he was nothing more than a hollow shell. Until there was nothing but raw pain to keep him upright.

Roughly, he turned away from the view he couldn't see, was blinded from seeing by his inner turmoil. He couldn't bear to see the azure pool where they had disported themselves, dazzling in the hot sunshine, the terrace they had lounged on, dined on, with candlelight catching her hair, the languorous warmth of the night like a caress…

He stalked indoors. He wanted out of here—as fast as he could.

'Are you done yet?' he demanded.

He didn't mean to sound curt, but impatience drove him. He was desperate to be on his way to the airport, to leave this place. He had to get to Hong Kong, then maybe Shanghai. He would do business there—profitable business. Because doing profitable business was what he did with his life, wasn't it? He made money. At first it had all been to bring down Grantham, but now it would be for its own sake. It was what he was good at, after all.

A sense of emptiness gaped in him. He'd achieved his goal—now what? What was he going to do with his life? What purpose was going to drive him now? There was nothing there for him. Nothing.

I thought I'd found what I was going to do with the rest of my life. And then she left me. Again.

Even though he'd been appalled to discover she was Grantham's daughter, dismayed by her taste in design, despite all that he'd come to terms with it. He'd made himself accept it because of the way he felt about her.

And she still rejected me.

Fernando was closing the lid of the large suitcase, fastening it securely. Then he straightened. 'What are your instructions in respect of the bracelet left in Miss Talia's room?' he enquired blandly.

Luke started. 'What do you mean?' he demanded. 'What bracelet?'

'I believe it is the one you had delivered yesterday,' Fernando elucidated.

Luke stared. 'The ruby bracelet?'

Fernando nodded in his stately fashion.

Luke frowned. 'She left it here?'

Again Fernando nodded.

Luke's face hardened. 'Send it on to her,' he said tersely.

He walked out of the bedroom, heading downstairs with a heavy tread. He had no idea why she'd left it—to make a point, perhaps? But what point? Why was *she* angry at *him*?

Perhaps it was insufficiently valuable?

His mouth twisted, his mood becoming blacker than black as he stalked out of the room, heading downstairs to the car waiting to take him to the airport. To take him anywhere in the world that was not this island where, for a brief space of time, he had thought he had found happiness.

What a fool he had been.

Well, never again. *Never again.*

Talia walked around the villa for the last time. It was empty now of all their possessions, right down to the kitchenware. Everything of value had been sold to raise some much-needed cash to tide them over. All Talia and her mother were taking with them were the bare necessities. It was all they could afford.

As she gazed about her Talia still could not believe what had happened since she had collapsed into desperate sobs on her mother's lap. When she'd finally stilled, the sorry tale told, her mother had been very quiet. At the edge of exhaustion—emotional, physical and mental—Talia had known, though she hadn't been able to face it, that she would have to cope with another complete collapse from her beleaguered mother.

Yet what had happened had been the complete opposite.

Maxine had finally patted her daughter's shoulder, and got to her feet. 'We,' she'd announced, 'are leaving. The moment we can. I will not stay for a day longer than it takes us to move out in *any* place owned by a man who has broken my daughter's heart. Nobody does that to my daughter. *Nobody!*'

That was all Maxine had said, but not all that she had done. She had conferred with Maria, returning to announce, with a straightening of her thin shoulders and an air of firm resolution, that Maria had come up with a *wonderful* solution to their dilemma.

'Her brother runs a café bar—not here in Marbella, down the coast in one of those tourist places. He needs someone to run it since he opened another one last month. And,' she continued triumphantly, 'it comes with an apartment above! We'll move in the minute we can.'

Talia had stared disbelievingly. This was not the mother she had known all her life. Nervy, brittle, and totally dependent on her daughter and husband.

'Mum, are you…are you sure you could cope?'

The change in lifestyle would be absolute. Terrifying, surely, for her mother?

Maxine's eyes had flashed. 'Yes,' she said simply. 'It's time—way beyond time—that I faced the truth about what has happened.'

Talia still couldn't believe the change in her mother, but she was abjectly grateful for it— and to Maria, who was giving them a way forward. It would be hard work, but right now—a choking sob tried to rise in her throat, but she pushed it back with determination—anything that blocked her mind from going where it kept trying to go was to be clung to with all her might.

Exhausting herself by running a café—waiting on tables, keeping it clean, doing everything except the cooking, which Maria's nephew was going to be doing—surely would leave her no time to think of Luke?

Please, God...

Luke flipped open the locks of his suitcase, intent on extracting a clean T-shirt to sleep in. Beyond the soundproofed windows in this most prestigious hotel in Hong Kong the glittering skyline of the city was like jewels glistening against the night. It was a city with millions of inhabitants, but he had never felt more alone in his life.

Emptiness gaped all around him.

Being on his own had become a way of life for him. He'd spent ten years focussed on making money and hunting down his enemy. There had been neither the time nor the inclination for relationships. His affairs—if they could even be called that—had been fleeting...strangers who met and parted again, never finding anything to keep them together.

For what woman would want to attach herself to a man as driven as he had been? As he had *had* to be in order to achieve what he had promised his parents he would do in their name?

But now that was all over. He was free—finally, blessedly free—to find someone to share his life with.

And I found her! I found her and wanted her and offered her everything I thought would make her want me too—

The cry came from deep within but he cut it off. There was no use listening to it. No use staring around this anonymous hotel bedroom and wanting, with a longing that was a physical pain in his gut, the one person who would make it the most wonderful place in the world for him.

She didn't want you. She left you.

He would force himself to stop wanting her. After all, she wasn't exactly the woman of his dreams, was she?

He knew what he was doing—that his mind was seeking ways to dull the pain by finding fault with Talia. But he forced himself to think of all the things that were wrong with her, to think about whose daughter she was, about what that had turned her into.

Do you really want to have a woman like

that in your life? A hothouse flower unable to survive without the shelter of a man to provide her with the luxuries of life, to look after her and cosset her? A woman who's only ever played at life? Who's never had to hold down a job, earn a living, work for what she has? Who's never had to take any responsibility? A show pony living off her father's wealth? Who panicked and collapsed when she was faced with losing her luxury lifestyle?

The questions seared in his head but he would not answer them. Dared not.

All he wanted now was a shower, a shave, and then to drink himself to oblivion from the bar in the room. Alcohol and sleep would silence the torment in his head. Because he was sure nothing else could.

He frowned. What the—?

On top of his neatly folded clothes was a large, stiff art folder. He stared angrily. Why on earth had *that* been packed? Talia's tasteless amateur daubs were the last thing he wanted to see!

Roughly, he yanked the portfolio out, flinging it onto the desk beside the suitcase stand. But he'd been careless in his aim, and as he fetched a clean white T-shirt the toilet bag in his hand caught the corner of the portfolio. It clattered to the floor, its contents spilling out.

With an oath, he stooped to scoop it all up, glad the sheets had fallen face-down. All except one, which he had to reach for.

He straightened, holding the sketch in his hands. Staring. Frowning.

Shock went through him.

This was no amateur daub. Nor was it anything remotely like any of the interiors he'd seen at the Grantham Land properties.

This was *good*! The vision was immediate, impactful. The wide space of the hotel's atrium was just the way it had been before the storm, but brought back to life in startling relief. He went on staring, taking it all in.

The deep cobalt-blue-tiled floor and the emerald-green walls made one vast fresco, bringing the lush rainforest indoors, splashed with the vivid colours of tropical flowers, of birds darting through the foliage with rainbow plumage. The huge arched opening to the terrace framed the gardens leading out to the sea, as azure as the tiling was cobalt, blending the interior with the exterior, making it one seamless whole.

And in his mind's eye it was instantly real— he could see it, *feel* it. Feel just what a newly arrived guest would experience on entering the hotel. It would stop them in their tracks.

There was no question this design had the total wow factor.

Mesmerised, he turned over the other sheets one by one, discovering what she had done for the restaurant, the bar, the bedrooms. All had been designed to have that same vivid, vibrant impact.

He spread them out on the desk, gazing down at them. Then he realised there was a transparent folder amongst them. Frowning again, he unfastened it to study its contents. There was an envelope of fabric swatches, each labelled carefully, and another envelope of downloaded illustrations from potential furniture, flooring, and fabric suppliers. And there, too, were multiple, neatly set out sheets—costings, prices, delivery schedules, names and contact details for suppliers and shippers, even notes about import licences and customs duties.

The information had been methodically researched and laid out, comprehensively covering all that would be required for him to make a decision on whether to go with her designs or not, and what it would cost him if he did. It was as thorough and as professional as her artistic vision was brilliant.

Numbly, he went on staring at Talia's work, his thoughts in chaos.

* * *

'Buenas tardes!' Talia smiled cheerfully at another customer arriving at the busy café.

She was glad it was busy because it gave her no time for thoughts of Luke. Run off her feet, she could keep her misery at bay. Only in the long reaches of the night, attempting to sleep on the settee in the sitting room of the tiny flat above the café, her mother in the single bedroom, would it devour her in muffled, useless sobs.

What use was crying? But that didn't stop her from doing it anyway.

Instead she must focus on her work: serving customers with drinks and relaying the dishes emerging from the kitchen, where Maria's nephew Pepe was in charge, and keeping an eye on her mother, who sat at a small desk off to one side and, to Talia's continuing astonishment, pored assiduously over the café's accounts.

'Darling, I'm good at accounts—you know I had to justify every penny I spent to your father!'

Talia did remember bleakly how her father had interrogated her own costings, brutally knocking off anything that he'd thought she'd overspent on, taking it out of the allowance he paid her instead of a salary.

But she shouldn't let herself think of that, because that made her remember how enthusiastically she'd worked out the costings for the ruined Caribbean hotel. Anguish tore at her—and not just for the waste of her efforts. For a reason so much more unendurable.

But endure it she must—and so she hurried back out to the pavement tables to take orders there.

The café was in a side street of this busy tourist town, with nothing to remind her of the showy glitz of Marbella and Puerto Banus. Which was why the logo on the side of a delivery van turning into the road caught her eye. It was that of an upmarket courier company she remembered from the days when expensive items had used to be routinely delivered to the Marbella villa.

The driver was getting out, looking uncertainly at the modest café. 'I am looking for Señorita Grantham,' he said to her, his voice doubtful. In his hand he held a small package.

Talia stared, then walked slowly forward. She took the package and signed for it with a confused frown. Her heart started to beat heavily, and on impulse she tore at the packaging. Then, as the tell-tale contents were revealed, confirmed by the glittering river of fire as she lifted the hinged lid of the box, she gave a cry of revulsion.

Slamming the lid back down, she dashed to the driver, who was climbing back into his van. *'Take it back!'* She thrust the package at him. 'I don't want it! Take it back!'

She whirled away, her heart slugging with a furious hammering. She bolted back inside the café, her face black with anger. Bleak with it.

That's all he ever thought I was: a silly, spoiled princess who wanted rubies from him.

The pain of it pierced her like a blade in her heart—her stupid, stupid heart.

Luke was in his office in Lucerne, sunlight bathing the high peaks visible from the windows. But he did not see them. His entire attention was focussed on what was being said to him on his phone.

'It was *refused*?' he snapped. 'And what the hell do you mean, the villa was empty? It can't have been!' He drew a sharp breath. 'Then where—?' He listened. *'What?* They were located *where*?'

He dropped the phone on to the huge mahogany desk, still staring, uncomprehending.

I told her she could stay another three months.

So why, when she had got exactly what

she'd come begging for, would she have vacated the villa after all? His frown deepened, lines indenting around his mouth grimly. And why the hell had she ended up in some dump of a café in a cut-price tourist town, waiting on tables?

Why leave the villa? Why end up in a dump instead? And why, above all, refuse the damn rubies I sent her?

That bracelet was worth thousands. To refuse it when she had been reduced to waiting on tables… It didn't make sense.

A space hollowed out inside him, as if a skewer had ground it from him.

But then, nothing about her made sense. Nothing at all.

Dimly, he became aware that his phone was ringing again, and he snatched it up. Only pre-screened calls came through on this line, so his PA must have cleared the caller. And when he answered it, he knew why. He listened with a gradual steeling of his body, his expression grim.

Then, as the call came to an end, he simply nodded. 'Good,' he said.

A single word. But in it was a wealth of meaning. More than ten years' worth of meaning.

He set the phone down again and crossed

to the window. He looked out across the lake to the cold snow-topped mountains beyond. The same snow seemed to be around his heart, inside his lungs. Memories from long ago pierced him—and a single word in his own mother tongue. A single name.

Nemesis.

Over ten years it had taken, and it had turned him from a carefree young stripling, full of eagerness for life and all that it could offer, to what he was now—to what he had become. An agent of the dark, unforgiving goddess of vengeance. Nemesis.

Justice, he tried to tell himself. Justice was more noble than vengeance.

He turned away, walked back to his desk, and threw himself into his chair, pressing his hands over the arms, his face set in steel.

Remembering.

Remembering what Grantham had done to his family had always been a kind of absolution for whatever sins Luke had committed in his pursuit of the man and his ill-gotten riches. But now, as his dark and troubled thoughts finally sank from his consciousness, another thought came.

His expression changed.

She needs to know.

He took a sharp, incising breath.

And I need to know, too.

To know why Talia had not stayed on in the villa when she'd begged him for it. Why she had refused the rubies he'd sent her to wait on tables instead.

His mouth tightened to a thin line.

And why I thought she hadn't a shred of talent or professionalism when what she produced is blazing with it!

But there was one question above all that he had to have the answer to—whatever it took to find it.

Why did she leave me?

CHAPTER TEN

TALIA WAS MOPPING the café floor, chairs piled on the tables, before finally closing up for the night. Pepe had left, her mother had long gone to bed, and Talia was yawning, too, tired as ever from the long working day.

Her glance went to the café's large windows. A car had drawn up outside—a long, low, luxurious black car. A car that suddenly, urgently, caused her to abandon her mop and dash over to shut and bolt the café door.

Too late.

He was getting out of the car and striding across the pavement to her as she fumbled with the locks and bolts. He effortlessly pushed the door open before she could get there. Stepped inside.

'I need to talk to you.'

Luke's voice was terse, his face grim. He'd known she was at this café, but to see her with a mop and bucket, swabbing the floor, had been a shock for all that.

She backed away—an instinctive, automatic movement. Shock was crashing through her—and so much more than shock.

'Go away! Leave me alone!'

Talia's voice was high-pitched and she stepped back from him, clutching at a table as if for support. Her legs were suddenly weak, the blood was drumming in her veins, and faintness was dimming her vision.

I can't bear for Luke to see me here. I can't bear to see him at all.

He was speaking again, stepping forward.

She tried to push past him, but his words stopped her.

'*Listen* to me—please. I have something important to tell you.'

'I don't want to hear it!' she cried out in that same high-pitched voice, shaking her head violently.

He ignored her. He had to say this—whether she wanted to hear it or not.

'There is something you need to know.'

Was that hesitation? Uncertainty.

She stared at him. Her heart was still thumping like a hammer in her chest. He was looking at her with an expression in his face she did not recognise. She could not get her brain into gear because all her senses were firing, overloaded with the closeness of him that was causing her lungs to seize and her breath to come in short pants.

He was speaking and she surfaced, finally hearing his words. She heard them, but could not take them in.

'Talia—your father is dead.'

She seemed to sway as the words reached into her consciousness. With an oath, he caught her arms, holding her upright, supporting her weight as faintness swept over her. He gently pushed her back and down, into a chair he yanked off a table, setting it upright for her to sink into on legs that were suddenly cotton wool.

Thee mou, he should have told her more gently. But to see her again, to have her there in front of him… The physical reality of her presence was still impossible to believe. And that was without the changes he could see— her hair scraped back off her face in an untidy ponytail, not a trace of make-up, wearing only a white shirt and a black skirt with an apron around it, the discarded mop behind her.

She was working like a skivvy and his brain

struggled to blend this with the spoiled little rich girl image he'd had of her for so long.

'How…how do you know?' Her voice was faint, her glistening eyes staring at the floor.

Luke hefted down another chair and sat himself on it. 'I've been searching for him,' he told her. 'Him disappearing as he did made it harder for me to complete the finer details of the takeover. And besides that—' He stopped.

Besides that I had to know what had happened to him…to the man I destroyed.

He took a breath. However bad this news for her, she had to give up on any hopes she might have that her father would come back to rescue her from a life of washing floors.

'How did he die?' She was still not looking at him, her voice remote.

'He…he fell from a hotel balcony in Istanbul.'

Her eyes lifted to stare at him. She had heard the hesitation in his voice.

'Fell?' She could feel her jaw tighten, to stop herself shaking.

Luke's lips pressed together thinly. 'An accident. That will be what the official report says. And it is best to keep to that.'

Her face contorted. 'Tell me the truth!' she demanded. Her eyes were like stones.

He took a heavy breath. If she wanted the grim truth, he would tell her. Why should she not know what her doting father had resorted to?

'Talia, in order to try and stave off financial ruin your father ended up borrowing money from some very unsavoury characters it was unwise not to repay.'

He didn't say more. Didn't need to. Whether Gerald Grantham had jumped or had been pushed, it came to the same thing.

He stood up. 'I didn't want you to hear it from the police—or read it in the newspapers first.'

She was looking at him, her expression masked. 'So you came to tell me in person?'

'Yes.' His own expression was as masked as hers, but inside him emotions were engaged in a savage dance.

'Well, you've told me, so now you can go.' Her voice was as expressionless as her face as she pushed herself to her feet.

Those emotions broke through the mask of his face. 'Talia, what the hell is going on? What on earth are you doing *here*?' He swept an arm around the café's interior.

Those stones were back in her eyes. 'That isn't your business, Luke. Nothing about me is your business.'

He took a step towards her, clasping her arms,

emotions surging in him, hot and unbearable to endure. 'Talia, *talk* to me—please. You owe me that, surely? After all we had together—'

Violently, she threw off his hands. 'Don't *touch* me!' she cried.

And then suddenly, from behind the bar, where there was a door to the upstairs apartment, came another voice. 'Get away from my daughter!'

Talia whirled around. Maxine was standing there, clutching her dressing gown to her thin body, her eyes sparking with fury. Two spots of colour burned in her cheeks.

'Mum, it's OK. He's leaving. He's leaving right now.' She turned back to Luke. 'Please go. Just go.' She spun back to her mother. 'Mum, please—it's OK. Go back upstairs. I'm just shutting up here. I'll be there in a minute. *Please!*'

But her mother was surging forward, bearing down on Luke where he stood, frozen.

'Get away from my daughter!' she cried again, her voice rising.

The cry was almost a shriek now, and Luke could see Talia's mother hyperventilating, her colour mounting. Then, horribly, with a strangulated gasp, she put a shaking hand to her chest. Clawing frantically, as if in hideous slow motion, Maxine collapsed.

'*Mum!*' Talia's voice was a scream, and then she was crouching down where her mother had folded, unconscious, onto the wet floor.

Luke pushed her aside. Talia gave another cry, but he thrust his mobile phone at her. 'Get an ambulance! *Now!*' he ordered.

Then he fell to work on her mother, lying mobile on the floor, seemingly lifeless.

He checked the pulse at her neck—*no pulse!*—then, ripping the lapels of the dressing gown aside, he found the end of her sternum and measured two fingers further up. He pressed one palm over the dorsum of his other hand and started a rhythmic pumping of Mrs Grantham's stricken heart as memory flooded through him.

Suffocating memory of knifing fear and horror.

'Is she going to make it?' Talia's stricken brain was trying to find the Spanish she needed. Whatever she'd said, the paramedics understood.

'We'll do our best,' they said, and then the ambulance launched forward, siren wailing, down the street.

Talia had no idea where the hospital was, and it seemed to take for ever to get there. But her mother was hanging on—just. The paramedics, when they'd arrived, had taken over CPR from Luke, applying defibrillation, then got her on to a stretcher, attached her to monitors. And now they were getting her where her mother's life might be saved.

And through that long, long night, as Talia sat by her mother's bedside in Intensive Care, the thread of life held still—though it was as frail as Talia's grip on her mother's hand was strong.

In the morning the cardiologist visited and carried out a careful examination. Her mother was to be kept under sedation, but it seemed, Talia was told, and she felt a relief so profound she was weak with it, that she would live. The CPR, instantly and correctly carried out, had saved her.

As Talia walked out into the reception area, numb with relief and exhaustion, Luke got up from a bench.

'How is she doing? They will tell me very little.'

Talia stared. 'Have you been here all night?'

He looked haggard. A thick growth furred his jaw and his eyes were sunken.

'What else could I do?' He took a breath. 'So, how is she?'

'She's pulling through,' she said, her voice hollow. 'She'll be kept in for some time, while she recovers from the operation, and then they want her to have some time in a convalescent home.'

'I'll arrange it,' Luke said.

Violently she shook her head. Her emotions were shot to pieces, in a thousand jagged fragments. 'Luke, this is none of your concern.'

She made to move past him. She had to get to the café to start work.

But her arm was caught.

'Talia, we need to talk—' Luke's breath caught. 'Especially now.'

She stared at him. Exhaustion, both of her body, from her long sleepless vigil by her mother's side, and her spirit from seeing Luke again, consumed her.

She shook her head wearily. She wanted to pull away from him, but she had no strength left. Numbly, she let him lead her out of the hospital and walked beside him, saying nothing, down to the sea front.

He sat her down on a bench on the promenade and then joined her. She moved away from him, to the end of the bench. It was an automatic gesture. To be here at all with him was hard to bear. To be close to him would be impossible.

Everything to do with him was impossible. *Impossible. Impossible. Impossible.*

The word echoed in her head—useless and pointless.

He doesn't see who I really am so everything is impossible.

She couldn't look at him—could only stare out over the promenade. The beach below was starting to fill up, parasols unfurling, tourists settling in for another carefree day of their holidays.

'Why,' she heard Luke ask, his voice grim, 'did you never tell me about your mother?'

Talia glanced at him, and then away. 'What relevance does that have?'

'That,' he retorted, 'is what I want to know.'

'It doesn't have any relevance,' she said.

'Did you know her heart was weak?'

She looked at him again. 'Yes.' Her eyes went out to the sea, so calm and still at this hour of the morning. 'It's why I wanted us to stay on at the Marbella villa for longer. She'd already been taken ill when I had to tell her we'd lost that, as well. She found it…difficult to cope.'

Her voice was stilted, reflecting her reluctance to speak. But she just didn't have the strength to oppose Luke right now. Exhaustion was uppermost in her mind. And an overwhelming level of emotion that she could not cope with. Not now.

She heard Luke swearing. It was in Greek, and it was low and vehement.

'And why,' he asked, 'did you not tell me that when you came to my offices to beg not to be evicted?'

Her head twisted. His voice was cold. Cold with anger. But anger was in her, too.

'Tell you *what*?' she spat. 'That the wife of the man you'd reduced to bankruptcy wasn't taking it too well? That she didn't like the fact that she wasn't going to have a lavish budget for topping up her designer wardrobe any longer? That she'd been reduced to nothing more than an eight-bedroom mansion with ten bathrooms, a swimming pool and a gourmet kitchen, on a millionaire's estate in Marbella, which she couldn't—oh, dear me, no—just *couldn't* bear to leave? Why didn't I tell you *that*?'

She saw his expression close at the violence of her tone.

'And what would you have done, Luke, if I'd told you all that? You'd have told me to get real. That our days of being pampered pets— her a queen and me a princess—were over! *I* knew that. But—' She stopped short.

She turned back to stare sightlessly over the Mediterranean Sea, dazzling in the sunlight, too bright to behold.

'But my mother couldn't face it. She was still clinging to hope. Still deluding herself with pointless illusions about my father sorting it all out and coming back to save us.'

And Mum's thoughts were as pointless as the illusions I wove about you, Luke—the illusions you tore to pieces when you made it clear what you thought of me.

She wrenched her mind away. What use was it to remember the illusions she'd so stupidly had about Luke? Clumsily, she got to her feet. She stood looking down at him where he sat, hands held loosely between his thighs. His head lifted. His expression was unreadable.

She gave a heavy sigh. It was all too much right now. Last night her mother had nearly died… And the man who had put the 'nearly' in that sentence was before her now. He deserved her gratitude, no matter how he had treated her.

'Luke, thank you. Thank you for what you did for my mother…' She took a difficult breath. 'At the café.'

He didn't say anything for a moment. Then, his expression bleak, he simply said, 'Don't thank me. If I hadn't turned up like that she probably wouldn't have collapsed.' Wearily, he lifted a hand to run it through his hair. He got to his feet. 'Talia—'

She shook her head violently. 'Luke, *no*! I can't take any more interrogation. I have to get back to the café. I have to start work.'

An oath broke from him. 'It's *absurd* that you should be working there!'

She lifted his hand from her arm, and even to touch him was unbearable. 'Luke, I *have* to go! I'm late. I have to open up the café.' She took a ragged breath and then said what it would cost her everything to say, but say it she must. 'I… I don't want to see you again. Please leave me alone.'

She didn't look at him. She could not. Instead, head bowed, she hurried from the promenade, diving into the narrow streets through which she could make her way towards the harbour and the café.

At the café, Maria's nephew was shocked at her news, and told Talia he'd get a friend to wait on the tables that evening and she must go to her mother. Gratefully, she conceded.

When she set off for the hospital at the end of the day she stopped off at the bank, checking to see if they could afford a week at a convalescent home to help her mother recover.

After that… Well, after that her mother would just have to recuperate in the apartment above the café. She sighed, but knew that anything else was out of the question. They just did not have the money for anything else.

Like a luscious but poisoned fruit, Luke's offer to pay her mother's nursing fees dangled in front of her. She thrust it aside.

I can't—I just can't. It would...

It would reduce her to what she would have become if she had stayed with him. What he thought she was—what he had always thought her—even when he'd held her in his arms. Pointless. Pathetic. A useless bauble.

She gave a muffled cry of pain and hurried into the hospital. It was no use to think of Luke or to agonise over what was in the past. No use at all. She must focus only on her mother—as she always had, all her life. And now, when she had come so close to losing her, her mother was more precious to her than ever.

A shiver went through her. In all her terror for her mother, and in all her personal anguish over seeing Luke again, she had hardly given the news Luke had brought her about her father a second thought. For a moment guilt went through her. Her father was dead—surely that should elicit some emotion from her? Some sense of grief?

Her face hardened. Her father had been nothing but a malign, controlling presence in her life. And in the life of her mother.

The life Luke saved!

Oh, she could tell herself that had Luke not come to the café as he had her mother might not have had her heart attack, but that did not take away the fact that it had been Luke's prompt action that had saved her.

Talia felt her heart constrict. For that she would be for ever grateful.

She was grateful too—abjectly so—that her mother, propped up on pillows, wired up to monitors and on a drip, could greet her with a weak smile. Talia hugged her carefully, closing her eyes in a silent prayer of thanks that she had not lost her.

But as she straightened her mother spoke in an agitated voice, one thin hand clutching at her daughter. 'Darling, that man! That dreadful man!'

Immediately Talia was soothing. 'Mum, he's gone, OK? He left. We won't be seeing him again.'

Even as she said the words she felt pain strike her. To have seen him again…to have had him so near…

Her mother's grip tightened. 'Darling, you mustn't go to him. Not after what you told me.'

Talia shook her head. 'He didn't come here to try and persuade me to go back to him,' she said heavily.

She paused, took a breath. She had to say this, and maybe telling her mother here in a hospital, where there was a crash team on hand if necessary, might be the safest thing to do? Her mother had changed so much since they had left the villa in Marbella. She had become strong and determined. Perhaps she could take this final blow as well? Talia could only pray so.

She took her mother's hands, held them in hers. 'Mum, Luke Xenakis came to see me to tell me...' She took another breath, then told her mother the grim news.

For her mother's sake, she kept to the official report that it had been an accident. Whether her mother believed it or not she would not press to find out.

Her mother listened, then loosed her hands to pick at the bedclothes, her gaze turning inward. 'I think I've known all along he would never come home. You were right about it from the start, darling.' Her voice twisted, became infused with pain and regret. 'He never cared about us at all. Not really.'

She looked at Talia, her gaze troubled.

'Never give your love to someone who does not—who *cannot*—love you back.'

Slowly, her eyes filling with tears, Talia bent to kiss her mother's cheek. Only two words sounded in her head.

Too late.

Desolation filled her.

CHAPTER ELEVEN

LUKE SAT OUTSIDE the hospital in the car he'd hired, his eyes peeled for Talia. He knew she was visiting her mother because he'd checked at Reception. In his head burned the one desperate question he must ask her. Only one—and he had to get an answer to it. However many times she told him to leave her alone, he needed to know why.

His expression was stark, his eyes focussed only on the brightly lit hospital entrance. And then suddenly she was there, head bowed, shoulders hunched, walking away. He gunned the engine, drew up alongside her and vaulted from the car.

She started in shock.

'Let me give you a lift. Talia—please. You look dead on your feet!'

She made to walk on, but he took her arm, feeling her tense instantly. He yanked open the passenger door and for a moment thought she would resist. Then, as if running out of energy, she sank down inside with a weary sigh.

Luke resumed his seat, moving the car off into the traffic. 'How is your mother?' he asked.

He kept his voice neutral. It was an effort, but he did it. To have her so close again, to catch her scent, to feel her presence pressing upon him, was torment.

She sighed, not looking at him. 'Improving, but still weak.' She swallowed, taking a difficult breath. 'I... I told her about my father.'

Luke's expression tightened. 'It will be hard for her—hard for you, too.' He didn't say any more.

Talia didn't answer, only closed her eyes. A weariness so profound she could not fight it any longer was sweeping over her.

'Why are you still here, Luke?' she heard herself ask tightly. 'I told you I didn't want to see you again.'

She heard the engine change gear and felt the car swing round to the left, heading inland. Her eyes flew open. 'This isn't the way to the café!'

'I know.' Luke's voice was grim. 'I need to talk to you, Talia.'

'There's nothing to say!' she cried. 'Nothing I want to hear from you!'

In the intermittent lights of the street, his expression was as grim as his voice. 'But there's a lot I want to hear from *you*, Talia. And I am not leaving Spain until I have answers.'

He pressed the accelerator and the car shot forward, picking up speed. Talia realised they were leaving town, heading up into the hills inland. A knot was forming inside her, but there was nothing she could do. Wearily, she sank back into torpor. The desolation she had felt at her mother's warning twisted inside her like snakes writhing.

The road started to wind, gaining height, and the outline of a *mirador* opened up before them. Luke slewed the car towards it, cut the engine. Far below the lights of the town pierced the night. Far beyond the sea glimmered beneath the rising moon.

He turned towards Talia. She wasn't looking at him, only straight ahead, her face unreadable in the dim light.

'I need to know, Talia, the answer to a very simple question.' His breath incised into his lungs. 'And you owe me an answer.' His jaw tightened and in his chest he felt his heart starting to thud heavily. 'Why did you leave me?'

Her head slewed round. Her face was expressionless. 'I didn't care for your offer, Luke.'

A frown flashed across his eyes. 'You prefer skivvying in a café?' There was open derision in his voice.

She gave no answer, and his expression twisted. Emotions were churning in him and he was fighting to keep them under control. He must not let them out—not until he had the answers he needed.

'I didn't care for your offer.'

Her words mocked him, echoing in his head. *So what offer* did *she want?*

'And why waitressing?' he pushed. 'Why not interior design?' He paused, then said what he knew he had to say. 'You're good, Talia. *Really* good. I was wrong to think otherwise— your designs for the hotel are stunning, and I want to use them for the refurb.'

For a second—fleetingly—he thought he saw something move in her eyes, but then it was gone. The same closed, tight expression was back. He could see that her hands were clenched by her sides.

But *why*? None of this made sense—none of it!

The words broke from him suddenly. 'None of this makes *sense*, Talia! Waiting tables when you could be using your talents—'

Something flashed across her face as her head whipped round. 'Which talent are you referring to, Luke? My interior design skills or being good enough in bed to be your mistress?'

'What?' Now the flash of black fire was in his eyes, not hers.

Her expression contorted and, like a dam shattering under impossible pressure, her self-control broke. She could take no more of this.

'You heard me. Tossing a ruby bracelet at me…telling me there was plenty more where that came from. What else did that make me but your *mistress*? Payment for services rendered.'

Luke's hands clenched over the steering wheel, an oath escaping him. 'That is *not* how I was thinking of you. I was simply trying to make it clear that I would look after you. That I understood—that I still *do* understand—just how hard it is for you without your father to look after you the way you're used to…the way he always did. That I would take his place—'

A noise came from her—a harsh, ugly sound that had shock in it and something more, too.

Horror.

Her eyes were sparking fury, her cheekbones stark against suddenly hollow cheeks as the breath was sucked out of her.

Emotion was running like a black tide in

him now, and it was unstoppable. He heard himself speaking again. The words bitten from him, each one as sharp as a dagger.

'It's taken me a long time, Talia, to forgive you for walking out on me after that first night without a word of explanation. Not until I discovered whose daughter you were did I understand why you'd walked. It took me a while to work out what I had to offer you to get you to be mine—the same luxury lifestyle you got from your father. *That's* what you went running back to—why you left me. That was the choice you made, wasn't it?'

She slewed round towards him, the suddenness of her movement cutting across him, and in her face was a fury that was like a blow across his cheek.

'No, it was *not*! It was *not* the choice I made! The choice I made, Luke, was the choice I have had to make *all my life*!'

Her features convulsed, and her eyes were pinpoints of anger. They skewered him like daggers. Her hands were fisted and he saw her lift them and bring them down sharply, vehemently, on the dashboard.

'You keep talking on and on about how I was a pampered princess, Daddy's doted-on darling! Showered with designer clothes and jewellery, given some toy job to preen my inflated ego, given a free deluxe apartment to live in, a flash car to drive. Everything a spoiled little brat could ever want. Well, I *was*, Luke. Yes, I *was* a pampered princess. But I lived in a *cage*, Luke.' Suddenly her voice was not vehement, but hollow, bleak. 'In a cage that had bars of gold that my father had welded around me. And I hated it.'

His lips thinned. The black tide was still running.

'You could have walked out, Talia, at any time. Made your own way in the world. You're a talented designer—you could have done real work...work you could have been proud of. You've shown you can with your designs for the hotel. Why didn't you have the guts to leave your gilded cage?'

She could hear the condemnation in his voice and a deadly familiar hollowness opened inside her. She let her hands fall limply to her lap again and slumped back in the seat. She ran a weary hand over her eyes. Tiredness ate at her. It broke her heart to be here with Luke, who was as harsh and as utterly uncomprehending as everyone else. He saw her the same way everyone else did.

Right from the very moment she'd walked into his office—when they'd both realised the coincidental connection between them—he had treated her as so much *less* than the person she knew she could be. The person she was in her heart—the one she wanted to be, tried to be. The person she thought he had seen that one incredible night when they had first met and again in their Caribbean paradise.

But all that time on the island this is what he thought of me. I worked so hard on my designs and he didn't even look at them. He was just working out how to buy me, how to drape me in jewels and fly me in jets to exotic places so he could own me, control me, just like my father. I thought he was offering me freedom, but he was just building his own gilded cage around me.

He would not understand, and she hardly knew why she was bothering to say it—knew only that she might as well, because she was here, now, in this car with him, high above the Costas, looking down from afar. Below, in the town, her mother was in the hospital. In a day or so she would move her out to a nursing home, and then back to the tiny apartment above the café. And she would go on working—waiting on tables, mopping floors, and getting by.

Luke would be gone. Back to his own life— a rich man's life that had nothing to do with her—and she would never see him again.

'No, Luke, I didn't have the guts to leave—

just as you say.' She heard herself sigh, defeat in every word. 'I only had the guts to stay.'

She didn't bother looking at him. What would be the point of that?

'I don't understand…'

There was an audible frown in his voice so now she did turn her head to look at him. A great weariness of spirit weighed her down.

She heard her voice answering him…weary, defeated. 'Luke, my father gave me everything, just like you said, but he made me pay for it. He made my mother pay, too. Oh, not in ways that anyone would notice, but we paid, all the same. We had to live our lives exactly as he wanted us to. We had to wear the clothes he wanted us to, live where he wanted, entertain the guests he wanted us to—had to be the ornaments in his hugely successful life that he wanted us to be. That was our purpose. To be his trophy wife and his trophy daughter.'

'And you were happy to do that.' Luke's voice was flat. Condemning still.

She could not make out his face, not in the dim light of the car's interior, but she knew it would have a closed, shuttered look on it. She should stop talking now, she knew, because he would not understand—could not understand. But she went on anyway.

'No.' A single word. And then. 'But my

mother was.' She shut her eyes. 'No one will ever understand, Luke, what goes on in the head of someone who is in thrall to a man who wants only to control every aspect of her life. I tried so hard, so often, to get her to see what my father was, but she kept blinding herself to it. My father knew it—knew I would never succeed, however much I longed to.' Her voice became bitter. 'And that became his way of controlling me, too. Because if I ever did anything that displeased him he would take it out on my mother. And then tell me that was what he had done. Any anger he had at her, from which she would flinch, and then make up endless pathetic justifications to excuse it, would be *my* fault! And if there was any attempt by me to break free of my cage, to exert my own will, my mother would suffer. My life was spent trying to reassure her, to soothe her jagged nerves, to calm her and support her— to protect her. I could never break free while she would be the one to suffer for it. And it takes courage to bear that, Luke. More than you know.'

Her eyes flashed open suddenly.

'And then that one night, at that party, I dared to take a risk that I had taken only once before.' Her face hardened now, with bitter memory. 'The only time before I had ever dared have a romance of my own, my father meted out punishment for it. Oh, not to me—to the man. My father got him sacked from his job and ruined his reputation so he would never get another in the industry. And then he told me exactly what he'd done. So that I would never do it again. It was his way of controlling me.'

Her face was stark, her eyes bleak.

'Even as you talked of escaping to the Caribbean I knew I could never take off with you, Luke. I couldn't abandon my poor, helpless mother, and I couldn't risk my father doing to you what he'd done to that young man. I knew nothing about you. I had no idea who you were. I knew only that you sported a fancy watch and stayed in an expensive hotel. But that would not have been enough to protect you from my father. His reach was long—he was a powerful man, and very, very rich.'

She gave a laugh—a hollow laugh that had no humour in it.

'And all along—' She took a ragged breath. 'All along you were poised to take over Grantham Land. *That* was why I was deluged with desperate texts from my mother that morning! My father had disappeared off the face of the earth, and now, of course, I know why. Because you were about to finalise the acquisition of everything he possessed, reducing my mother and me to absolute penury. Penury that made me go begging to you, that made you think of me as you do.' Her voice twisted with a savage bite. 'That made you think that all I craved was to be your bejewelled and pampered bird in a cage.'

That hollow half-laugh broke from her again, then stopped abruptly. 'How ironic does life get, Luke? Tell me that. You've turned out to be just another rich, ruthless bastard like my father!'

She heard an oath escape him in his native Greek. Its tone was harsh, crude, and ugly, though she could not understand its meaning. Then he was hurling words at her, in Greek and then in English, his eyes burning with a savage fire.

'I am *nothing* like your father! *Nothing* like the man who killed *my* father!'

A razored intake of air seared Luke's lungs like a heated blade. Emotion convulsed in him. He rounded on her, staring at her, but it was not Talia he was seeing. His gaze was into the past.

He began to talk.

'My father owned a hotel—small, but beautiful. It had been his grandfather's house, right by the sea, a haven of peace and tranquillity set in olive groves on an island in the Aegean. To my parents it was everything and they loved it dearly, dedicated their lives to it. But...'

His voice grew shadowed. 'When I was a student, an earthquake hit and the hotel was badly damaged. They could not afford to restore it. So...' He paused. 'So when a wealthy investor—an Englishman—offered them financial help, they could not believe their good fortune.'

He paused again.

'My parents were simple people. Naive in many ways. Dangerously so, you could say. They trusted this eager, enthusiastic Englishman and signed the paperwork he set in front of them, believing they had years to repay their debt out of future hotel profits. It seemed a fair deal.'

He could see Talia's expression changing. He went on remorselessly.

'But your father did not believe in fair dealing. What he believed in was profit—made any way he could. And what he saw in my parents' place was not a small boutique hotel but the valuable land it stood on—shoreline, beachfront.' He paused yet again. 'Ripe for development.'

Luke's mouth twisted.

'You won't need me to spell out what was on the paperwork that my parents so gratefully signed—a contract giving your father total control over the rest of the land. It let him bring in chainsaws to demolish the olive groves, bulldozers to flatten the terrain, teams of construction workers to build a massive high-rise monstrosity of a hotel right beside my parents' hotel, dwarfing it, destroying all its charm, its beauty. It was ruined financially for ever. And then, when my parents were unable to repay any of the money he'd lent them, he simply foreclosed on them. He took everything from them. *Everything.*'

He realised his hands were still clenched around the wheel, as if moulded to it. Forcibly, he lifted his fingers away, flexing them. He looked away from her, out at the coastline far below.

'Do you know the reason I knew how to do CPR on your mother? Because I made myself learn.'

His voice had changed again, and in it was something that struck fear into Talia,

'I had to watch my own father collapse and die of a heart attack in front of my eyes because of what your father had done to him. Your father caused his death as surely as if he'd plunged a knife into his chest himself.'

His head snaked to face Talia.

'Your father was doomed the day I buried mine. I vowed to ruin him, to bring him down. And, yes, the night of that party was the very night I'd finally acquired the means to do so. After ten gruelling years of turning myself from student to tycoon, forcing myself to build the fortune I knew I'd need to destroy him, I finally acquired a sufficient shareholding to take over Grantham Land.'

For a long moment Talia was silent. Then she spoke with a heaviness that was crushing her. 'I walked back that morning into a cage that was no longer there. But I did not know it.'

He didn't answer. The silence between them stretched. Then, 'And if you *had* known it?'

His voice was so low she could scarcely hear it. She shut her eyes. They were hot suddenly, and burning, and she could not bear that either.

'What does it matter, Luke?'

The weariness was in her bones. To know that Luke had been as much a victim of her father as she had been, that he had wreaked havoc on his parents' lives as he had on so many other lives, could make no difference.

'What does it matter?' she said again. 'Any more than it matters why I walked out of the gilded cage *you* offered me in the Caribbean!'

Her hands convulsed in her lap.

'I thought I had been given a second chance out there on the island with you. I knew that wherever my father was he would not be coming back—and that meant my mother and I were penniless. But it also meant that I could take my chance of finding happiness.' Her voice was sad as she stared down at her hands. 'Discovering what you thought of me ripped that stupid illusion from me.'

She made herself look at him. Forced herself. It hurt to do so, and not just because of the pain that she was fighting to ignore pricking behind her eyes. It hurt to see the planes of his face, the hard edge of his jaw, the deep darkness of his eyes that had no expression in them at all as he met her gaze.

Something cried out inside her, but she tamped it down. 'I'm sorry, Luke,' she said, her voice still heavy. 'I'm sorry that I am the daughter of the man who did so much harm to you. I'm sorry I abandoned you that first morning after the party. I'm sorry I don't want to be your mistress. I'm sorry—'

She broke off. His hand had shot out and crushed down on hers, silencing her. Greek broke from him again, vehement and urgent.

'*Thee mou,* do you think I *wanted* you to be a pampered princess who expected a life of luxury? Corrupted by your father's wealth so that you'd crave it in any man you might choose to replace him with?' He took a ragged, scissored breath. 'Don't you *know* what I want? What I have wanted from the moment I set eyes on you?'

He closed his other hand around hers, lifting it to his cheek. His fingers were warm around hers but her hand lay still, as if paralysed. The same paralysis held her motionless, stilling the breath in her lungs, the set of her gaze on his face.

'I knew I shouldn't want you—not after you walked out on me that morning. Not after you revealed yourself as the daughter of my enemy. Not after you begged me to let you keep the villa in Marbella that I thought you felt entitled to. Not after I succumbed to the temptation to take you to the Caribbean, telling myself it was to make you work and earn the right to stay on in the villa.'

His voice grew heavy now—with self-condemnation.

'Not even when I told myself, as you lay in my arms, that I should make allowances for you being a hot-house creature who could not survive without luxury and someone to look after you all the time. I *knew* I shouldn't want a woman like that.'

He halted, and Talia felt his strong fingers spasm suddenly over her limp hand.

'But I did,' he said. 'God help me, I did.'

Abruptly he let her hand drop, turned away again. The cramped confines of the car were claustrophobic suddenly. On an impulse he could not control he threw open the door and vaulted out. He stood in the mild night air, with the moon sailing serenely overhead, the chorus of cicadas in the vegetation all around raucously audible. For him there was only the hectic beating of his heart. Like blows against his chest.

Grimness possessed him.

He had got her wrong. So, so wrong.

He heard her get out of the car as well and take a few steps over the gravel to stand beside him. He tensed at her approach. Heard her speak.

'And *I* knew,' she said, with strain in her voice, 'that I should not want a man who thought so ill of me…' She paused. 'But I did.' She paused again. 'I *do*.'

For the space of a heartbeat he did not move. Then slowly, infinitely slowly, he turned towards her.

'It cost me so much to leave you that first morning, Luke—after the party. But I had to do it for my mother's sake. And it cost me even more to leave you when I did on the island. But I had to do that for *my* sake. Because if I'd stayed it would have destroyed me—day by day, night by night. Knowing what you thought of me...what you believed me to be. What I would have become. A woman in love with a man who despised her.'

She made to turn away, but Luke stopped her with a hand on her arm.

'*What* did you say?'

He stepped towards her, and as Talia stared up at him she saw his expression change in the moonlight.

'You said,' he told her, and now there was something in his voice that went with the expression on his face, 'that you would have been "a woman in love"?'

Tears, hot and anguished, pricked her eyes now, breaking away from the control she'd pressed them back with.

'I shouldn't have said that, Luke. We have nothing else to say to each other now.'

'*Yes!* Yes, we *do*!' Luke's voice cut across hers. Vehement and urgent. 'After everything we have finally said to each other we haven't said the one thing that really matters.'

He took a breath, his eyes directed at hers.

'Right from the very first time I set eyes on you I knew, with every instinct in my body,

that you were special. It had nothing whatsoever to do with the goal I had finally achieved,
the destruction of the man who had destroyed
my parents. I was finally free of that burden—
finally free to choose how to live my life. Free
to *choose*, Talia.' He took another breath, his
eyes never leaving her for an instant, a heartbeat. 'Free to fall in love…'

He heard her give a little cry, but he could
not stop.

'Had you come with me after our first night
together I would have fallen in love with you
then.'

He saw the tears spilling from her eyes,
catching the moonlight, and then his arms
were around her, drawing her to him. He felt
his heart soar in his chest.

'Forgive me, I beg you,' he said, his arms
tightening, 'for all the ill I thought of you.
I will strive with all my strength to make
amends for it—to be worthy of your love!'

He felt her arms tighten around him, clutching at him, felt her shoulders heave with sobs,
and then he was cradling her tear-stained face
with his hands, his eyes soft and cherishing.
His mouth grazed hers in tender homage.

'Don't cry. Never cry again. I honour everything about you—your loving loyalty to your
mother, your courage in sticking by her, not

abandoning her to your father's wrath just to gain your own freedom. I honour you for the strength and courage you've shown in protecting her after your father's ruin, whatever the cost to you. And I honour, above all, the choice you made in leaving me—both that very first morning and when you left me in the Caribbean after I got it so, so wrong about you.'

'I was scared!' she cried, remembering her mother's words to her in the hospital. 'Scared I would repeat what she had done. That I would stay with a man who treated me with contempt—who never loved me.'

He kissed her again. 'Love me as I love you…and if you do then you will love me.'

His smile seemed to melt away the harsh words that had passed between them and turn her heart over.

'I love you to all the reaches of infinity.'

She broke into renewed sobbing and he let out a laugh, swirling her around in his arms, lifting her feet off the ground in the moonlight. Then he lowered her gently, tenderly, back to the ground.

'Weep all you want,' he said softly. 'For when you have done I never want you to weep again.'

He shut his eyes momentarily, filled with an emotion he could barely contain, and then they sprang open again as he put his arm around her and they turned together to face the view of the town, the coast and the horizon beyond. A great quietness settled over him…a peace of the heart.

'We're finally free,' he said quietly. 'Free of what your father did to both of us. Free to live our lives as we wish. Free to love as we wish. And even free,' he finished wryly, 'should we wish it, to avail ourselves of my suite at my hotel! It's a beautiful place up in the hills. An old Moorish fort with fabulous views over the coast.' His hand tightened over hers. 'Will you come with me? Stay with me this time?'

Her smile was all he needed to see. And the softening of her gaze with a light that outshone the moon.

'I'll never leave you again, Luke,' she said. *'Never.'*

It was a promise. A vow. To him, and to herself.

EPILOGUE

'So, WHAT DO you think, Mum?'

Talia swept an arm around the circular atrium with its cobalt floor and its walls muralled in vivid emerald, with foliage and crimson flowers, wide arches opening to the glorious gardens beyond.

'You've got an incredibly talented daughter,' said Luke, and smiled, standing beside her.

Talia's mother clapped her hands. 'Oh, darling, it's *wonderful*!'

The man beside Maxine grinned. 'Pretty good, Talia.' He nodded. Then he glanced at Luke. 'When's the grand opening?'

Luke helped himself to Talia's hand. 'Right after our wedding,' he said. 'Until then we're keeping it private—just for family. Talia and I are going to test-drive the open-air chapel out on the promontory. Shall we go and take a look now?'

'Oh, Luke, yes!' Maxine cried. She cast a

look at the man beside her. 'And maybe after you two have tied the knot,' she said lightly, 'Mike and I might try it out too!'

Talia's expression lit up. 'Oh, Mum! That would be *brilliant*!'

She cast a warm look at the man beside her mother. Easy-going, weather-beaten, with a piratical beard. He was dressed in cut-off denims and a striped top—the uniform of a seafaring yachtsman—and he was the very antithesis of her father.

She could not have been gladder of it. Already, in the nine months since she and Luke had gone to see her mother in the hospital and told her of their love for each other, her mother had bloomed. And then Mike, who had one day moored his boat off the hotel jetty, had taken one look at Maxine, who had been visiting the island, and recognised in her a teen romance from their youth and stayed to rekindle it.

Now, as the four of them made their way through the restored atrium out on to the terrace beyond, and then along the pristine pathways, there was no sign at all of the devastation that the hurricane had caused.

Talia felt her heart swell with happiness. She leant into Luke. 'How can I be so happy?' she breathed.

He smiled down at her, his eyes warm with love. 'Because you deserve it,' he told her, and dropped a kiss on her forehead.

He led her out on to a small grassy promontory, where a ring of palm trees swayed in the constant breeze, lifting the heat. A thatched open air chapel, with seating in front was set out there. They paused while Mike and Maxine caught them up, and then they all turned back to look at the hotel, fully restored now, after months of endless work.

Again, Talia felt her heart lift. 'We've made it *so* beautiful again!' she exclaimed.

'It deserves to be,' Luke said. He looked down at Talia again, squeezing her hand. 'And I know why I was so determined to save it.'

There was a thread of sadness in his voice that made Talia squeeze his hand in return, to comfort him.

'Because what is broken can be restored, with enough time and enough love—buildings, people, relationships...'

'You saved it for your parents' sake,' Talia said in a low voice. 'And I'm glad—*so* glad.'

Luke turned her gently towards him. 'Will you truly be happy, getting married here on this spot?'

Her eyes lifted to his, shining with the sun. 'How can you even ask?' she said. 'I would be happy marrying *you*, my darling, darling Luke, anywhere in the whole wide world! For you are my heart, Luke. My whole heart.'

He lowered his mouth to hers. Peace filled him. Peace, thankfulness and love. Always love. And love embraced him as he embraced the woman he loved…embraced them both for ever.

* * * * *

If you enjoyed
Irresistible Bargain with the Greek
you're sure to enjoy these other stories by Julia James!

The Greek's Secret Son
Tycoon's Ring of Convenience
Heiress's Pregnancy Scandal
Billionaire's Mediterranean Proposal

Available now!

4460

to do this afternoon. There were Luke's letters
to type up first.

The office she was shown into by the stately
butler—whose name, he informed her upon
enquiry, was Fernando—was chilled with air-
conditioning and had no outside light coming
in. The windows were high set, with venetian
blinds over them. An array of high-tech equipment hummed to one side, and a huge PC sat
on the desk.

She took her place in front of it and got out
her notebook. She sighed, hoping she would
be able to decipher what she'd scrawled so
hectically.

It proved hard going, and she knew, with a
sinking heart, that she was making a poor fist
of it. She did her best, all the same, though
she was painstakingly slow, not being able to
touch-type, and found the keyboard complicated to operate when it came to tabulating the
many figures Luke had thrown at her.

Finally, she was done, though there were
gaps and queries in every letter and attachment. She could only hope that Luke would
make allowances for the fact that she was not
a trained secretary and they had been going
over a bumpy road while she was trying to
write it all down.

The headache, which had cleared over lunch

in the fresh air, was now back with a vengeance. With a final sigh of abject relief, she closed down the word processing software and got up, her back stiff and sore from hours of hunching over the keyboard.

Then her face brightened.

The pool! She would freshen up with a dip—that, surely, would clear her head and loosen her stiff limbs. And she would ask the Fernando if she could have a coffee, and a long juice drink.

A handful of minutes later she was plunging head-first into blissfully warm water, joyfully dipping her head under the water to feel her hair stream wetly down her back. Her spirits soared. Oh, this was joyous! She splashed around, frolicking like a child, delighting in the diamond sprays of water catching the late-afternoon sunshine, then pushed off the side, plunging in a duck-dive to the tiled bottom of the pool, dappled with sunlight. Then:

'What the *hell* do you think you're doing?'

CHAPTER FIVE

THE STENTORIAN VOICE halted Talia mid-plunge and she floundered back up. Her eyes went to the edge of the pool as she brushed the strands of wet hair from her face.

Luke was standing there, glowering down at her. Talia blenched, grabbing the edge of the pool to steady herself. 'I… I wanted a swim,' she said.

She didn't try to make her voice sound defiant—let alone entitled—but Luke seemed to take it that way. She could tell by the instant darkening of his eyes.

'May I remind you,' he bit out, and the sarcasm was blatant in his clipped words, 'that you are here to work. This is *not* a holiday for you!'

She saw him breathe in sharply, lips pressing in a thin line.

Talia opened her mouth to tell him she knew that, and understood it only too clearly, but he forestalled her attempt at self-defence.

'What's happened to those letters I left you to type up?' he demanded.

'I… I've done them. That's why I thought it would be OK to have a swim,' she said falteringly.

Clumsily, she hurried to get out of the pool, wading up the steps. As she emerged she was burningly conscious that, even though she was wearing a plain one-piece suit, it was clinging to her body, exposing every curve and a lot of bare leg. She seized a towel and wound it round her body while her wet hair streamed water down her back.

His eyes were on her, she could tell, and she felt colour flare out across her cheeks as she dipped her head, squeezing water out of her long hair. She hoped he would go, so she could escape up to her room, but he was not done with her yet.

'My PA said she's received nothing,' he retorted.

She looked confused. 'You didn't say anything about sending them anywhere. And I don't have any contact details.'

He cut across her. 'It will have to be done *now*.' His mouth tightened. 'Get changed and meet me in the office.'

He strode off before she could make any reply, and disappeared indoors. Hurriedly,